TAINTED
MOONLIGHT

ERIN KELLY

♡ Enjoy☺

Erin Kelly

TAINTED MOONLIGHT Copyright © 2016 Amy E. Baker / Erin Kelly

For more information and the latest news on the Tainted Moonlight series, check out the official website: www.taintedmoonlightbook.com

Website design and layout © Jennifer Winford / Tiny Dog Media
www.TinyDog.me

Cover art features the image "Moon Over the Dome" and is used courtesy of and in collaboration with Everet D. Regal. Original photograph is © Everet D. Regal and used with permission. To order a print of the original image and for more amazing photography please check out his full gallery at

http://everet-regal.pixels.com/

This is a work of fiction. All of the characters, organizations, and events portrayed in this novel are either products of the author's imagination or are used fictitiously. Any existing local businesses or parks portrayed the author encourages you to check out, and have not paid for promotion in this book.

ISBN: 1535034289
ISBN-13: 978-1535034289

DEDICATION

This first one goes out to my dear friend- more like my pack sister really- Samantha, who first helped me unleash the wolves years ago. This story would not exist without you. Thank you for your support through the years, most of which I can never truly thank you enough for. Our Lobo wouldn't be who he is today without you.

CONTENTS

1: JOB INTERVIEW WITH A WEREWOLF

"Mr. Diego, can you tell me what it's like being a lycanthrope?"

Korban blinked, staring at the thin hiring manager who was eagerly returning his gaze from behind a large pair of glasses. He couldn't have heard him right. "I'm sorry?" he managed an amicable smile to the nice man who sat across the desk.

"Tell me what it's like to be a werewolf," he repeated, eyes bright and eager.

The internet didn't exactly cover this kind of question during a job interview. Then again, up until five years ago even the internet believed werewolves to be only something in myths and bad horror flicks. Korban averted his gaze to the polished desk, the shiny name plate greeting him with the name Brett Kensington. Of course the topic would come up about his... condition. His eyes were a dead giveaway; no longer the chocolate brown of his mother's but now a constantly wolf-like amber that nearly glowed with the pull of the full moon, which happened to be that night.

He looked up again and decided to answer this offbeat question. He really needed this job. "As a werewolf I am physically stronger and faster than I was before I was bitten. I can easily lift about three to four times my weight, maybe more with practice. I am not available to work the night of the full moon for obvious reasons, and the morning after I need time to recover. Otherwise I am just as capable as any other candidate, maybe even more so because of my strength." There, that was a pretty reasonable response that put a positive spin on what could have taken a negative turn.

"What about your eyesight? Your hearing? All the senses?" Brett was taking notes, scribbling on a yellow legal pad.

He wasn't sure how it mattered working in a steel foundry but offered another smile. "My eyes and ears are more sensitive, but it won't affect my work. My sense of smell is incredible, but I've grown used to it as well." He wondered why he'd bothered listing his credentials and skills on his resume.

"Interesting," he paused for a moment then asked, "How long ago were you bitten?"

"Five years ago this fall," he felt very uncomfortable answering these sort of personal and invasive questions. He had survived a werewolf attack and he remembered it as clearly as if it happened yesterday. The nightmares of a giant black wolf ripping into his throat in a dark alley still haunted him. He shifted in his chair.

"Do you feel that you have good control over your wolf-side?" Brett peered at him curiously.

Perhaps this had something to do with the job? Maybe he was legitimately curious about it, to make sure this wouldn't affect his relation with other employees. "I have two roommates that help me stay locked down during the full moon. One of them is my sponsor and the reason I am free to be here today, and not stuck in quarantine." Like so many of the others, who weren't as lucky as him, he thought but did not add. He *really* needed this job. "I honestly don't remember what happens once I black out during the shift, but I have never harmed anyone, thankfully."

"I see, I see," Brett tapped his pen thoughtfully on the paper, the sound welcome to cover up the wet thumping sound of his heart. "What's the transformation like? Is it painful?"

"With all due respect, sir, what does that have to do with this job?" Korban asked levelly, trying not to reveal his growing anxiety or anger in his tone. He was done with these prying questions.

The manager folded his hands, then steeples his fingers together. For a moment the clock ticked on the Rolex around his small wrist. "Mr. Diego, I have a proposition for you."

Finally down to business. "Okay," he straightened up in his chair.

"I want to become a lycanthrope."

Korban stiffened, surely not hearing him right. "Excuse me, *what?*"

"I want you to bite me. I want to become like you," Brett spoke quickly, leaning across his desk. "Not for free of course. I'll compensate you generously for your time and effort."

"Whoa, whoa," Korban held up his hands in protest, "you want me to *infect* you? I'm sorry, I can't do that- that's an automatic death sentence in New York." Along with many other states, some of which had even stricter laws- the shoot-first-and-ask-questions-later sort of rules.

"You'll be generously compensated, and the transaction will be completely confidential. Name your price and I'll put it through, a discreet transaction in a numbered account somewhere that doesn't tax. I want this, Mr. Diego. I'm not going to call the police."

This had to be some sort of joke, he wondered if there was a

3

camera crew waiting beyond the door, ready to pounce. He swallowed thickly, loosening his tie to get more air. It felt more like a choke chain than professional attire to the wolf. Inside he was already reeling, the wolf in him wanting to flee this danger, or turn and fight, and he couldn't have that. "You have to understand, Mr. Kensington. I didn't choose this. I wouldn't wish this on my worst enemy, believe me. It's not just super strength and speed, it's teeth and claws and unimaginable pain every month. Worse, it's losing an entire night to something you can't control, something that isn't you that lurks inside, something dark always under the surface. A beast that's caged within you and lashes out whenever you're at your weakest."

Brett gave a flippant wave of his hand. "I've done my research. This is what I want, and you can provide it to me. This is just the beginning, a sign on bonus if you will. Now do we have a deal Mr. Diego," he slid a check with a lot of zeroes trailing a one across the desk, "or not?"

Korban met Brett's anxious gaze. It finally sunk in. "You didn't call me in for a job here, did you?"

"I'm afraid this company isn't hiring, but you won't need a job at all if you accept my offer. Retire young, maybe move someplace where the weather isn't bipolar year round. You must admit, it's an enticing offer."

He snorted. "Yeah, try travelling when everyone you pass on the street considers you a monster. Don't you watch the news? Being a werewolf isn't what it's cracked up to be. What you see in books and movies, it's nothing like that. This is real. You get shot if you're outside past curfew-"

"*If* they catch you," Brett emphasized.

"I'm fast, but there's no way I'm faster than a speeding bullet.

I'm no superhero." Korban paused, then attempted to make his own point very clear. "They treat me like I'm the villain. Curfews, quarantine, restrictions. Do you have kids, Mr. Kensington? I can't even go fifty yards near a school. They treat us worse than pedophiles."

"So you won't do it then."

"No, and I've wasted enough time here." Korban stood quickly, not even bothering to shake the man's hand. He pulled his sunglasses from his pocket and slid them on as he headed for the door, while the man made his final attempts to persuade him.

"Mr. Diego, if you don't do this I'll find someone who will! Someone who'll take me up on this once in a lifetime offer!"

He paused, his hand on the doorknob. He didn't bother to turn around. He could smell the last thread of hope grow in the man behind him. "I hope you realize what you're getting in to before you make that mistake." He quickly fled the room, careful not to slam the door too hard behind him.

Korban was all too grateful to make it outside the stuffy office building. He loosened his tie, glancing up to the darkening sky, suddenly aware of the time. Twenty minutes until curfew, about thirty or so to the transformation. He'd wasted far too much time arguing with that lunatic who'd wanted him to bite him. The thought that someone would want this life made his stomach churn. He made his way quickly to the bus stop, only to catch the familiar stench of oil and exhaust fading away. Korban swore and began to jog up the street. There was enough time to get back home if he hurried on foot.

Luckily his speed was no exaggeration, but unfortunately even he could not out race the clock. He was still a few blocks away when curfew hit. The wail of the sirens in the distance made him pick up the pace even more, his muscles on fire from the moon rising in the sky and the rush of adrenaline coursing in his veins. He caught a glimpse of red and blue lights flickering up ahead and he darted into an alley, flattening himself against the wall. He closed his eyes, listened to the grind of gears in the engine, the rubber tires rolling against a pothole in the road, and then the sound faded away as the police car continued its patrol down the road. His heartbeat pounded and echoed in his head as he strained to hear if the coast was clear. There came a sharp pain deep in his stomach, causing him to hunch over and gasp. There wasn't much time left.

Panting, he leaned against the cool brick wall and gazed up to the darkening sky. The moon was rising over the thick cover of clouds along the horizon, the pressure radiating through his bones. Jerking his head away he took off running, full speed towards the garage. Crossing a side street a horn blared and tires squealed, but he leapt out of the way of the car and continued to move like a blur towards his destination, the familiar worn garage up ahead.

The weather-beaten sign read CYRUS AUTOS. The solid garage doors already were closed for the evening. He burst through the side door and slammed it behind him, quickly latching the set of locks that sealed others out, and more importantly kept him in. The force of the door slamming rattled the tools and assorted collection of items along the wall, including a small array of colorful, plastic pinwheels which slowly spin in the wake of him rushing in. A cramp shot through his stomach and he nearly fell over, knocking down a few tires that were stacked near the entrance. He wrenched his tie away from his throat, trembling hands loosening his belt. He managed to step out of his pants and shoes as the pain escalated to something unbearable and he collapsed to the ground, curling into himself. Pain stabbed through him and he abandoned his struggle to unbutton his sweat-soaked shirt. He'd run out of time.

He remained on the floor in agony as his bones and muscle

twisted impossibly, yielding to the beast caged within him. His skin burned and itched as fur sprouted thick and damp with his sweat. His jaw and nose stretched and his acute sense of smell stung with the familiar scent of oil and brick and metal. For a fleeting moment he heard the wolf's thoughts. *My territory. Home.*

Then he was lost to the beast, the wolf springing free as he finally lost consciousness.

~*~

When Korban woke his mouth was dry and he could taste something sickeningly metallic on his tongue.

He panicked for a split second as he wondered, *Blood?* Then his eyes focused on the worn and chewed hubcap laying in front of him and he groaned.

The morning after a full moon was like the worst hangover imaginable. Beyond reaching the garage and succumbing to the moon's painful embrace, he had no memory of the night before. His head and body ached from being contorted and bent through the transformation, and all of his senses were dulled down to normal once again, making him feel blind and stuffy compared to the night before. Now to top it all off his mouth tasted of scrap metal.

He could see his human reflection in the remaining smooth parts of the mangled piece of metal. His yellow eyes were weary and bloodshot, the supernatural color a constant reminder that he wasn't fully human anymore. His tanned skin, dark eyebrows and the dark fall of his bangs... everything was back to normal, but seeing his own familiar reflection was a relief.

"Morning Sleeping Beauty!" An all-too cheerful voice chimed from above, and he glanced over and watched as his friend trotted down the stairs and dropped a blanket over his head. Alejandro Cyrus was one of Korban's roommates and like a brother to him, and the current owner of the garage. In the years he had known Alex he hadn't changed all that much- just growing a little taller through the years. Even with his vision hidden under the fleece cloth of the blanket Korban knew Alex's brown eyes were sparkling with mischief, his dark hair mostly hidden under a backwards baseball cap, and his grin a dazzling, devilish smirk. Alex never failed to deliver when it came to clever remarks, whether you wanted them or not. True to form, Alex adds, "Er... wrong fairy tale."

Korban yanked the blanket down and saw his friend's grin widen as he spotted the now useless tire cover lying beside him. "I see you had a good time last night."

"Good morning to you too, Alex," Korban rolled his eyes, unable to think up a witty response this early in the morning. He would get him back after breakfast.

Alex carefully picked up the scrap metal and frowned. "I don't see what everyone's problem is with werewolves. Maybe they have expensive rims to protect?"

Despite himself, Korban chuckled, wrapping the blanket around himself. He caught the smell of eggs, bacon and coffee wafting from upstairs and his stomach growled. He watched Alex study the chewed hubcap and then carefully hang it on the tool wall. "I'll hold on to your new chew toy for next time."

Next time. A month from now when the full moon returned to torment him, to remind him that he wasn't normal anymore. He wasn't the only one cursed, and the curfew every full moon night was a reminder. The problem was he didn't know how many others faced the full moon in terror, knowing the pain and what they would become. The only other werewolf he had met had practically torn his throat out and cursed him to face the same monthly ritual. The thought of running into another one like him was terrifying. He preferred being locked in the safety of the garage, away from anyone or anything that boldly roamed during a full moon night.

He got up on his feet, the blanket draped around him as he sought the remnants of his suit to salvage. He grit his teeth but made no outward signs that he was in pain as he gathered up his scattered clothes then made his way upstairs to the apartment while Alex started to set up shop for the day. Alex joking with him, teasing him was okay- but he didn't want his pity.

Korban made his way upstairs to the small two bedroom apartment that was above the garage, the smell of breakfast luring him towards the table where his other roommate was quickly skimming over the newspaper. He deposits his clothes into the hamper as RJ turns to him. If Alex was like a brother, RJ was definitely the big brother of the trio. Perhaps even a father figure, which RJ resembled in his suit and tie ensemble, a steaming mug of coffee in his hand and the morning paper spread out on the table before him.

While Alex was the joker, RJ had been the caretaker of the three of them since Alex's grandfather, a man the entire neighborhood knew as Pops, passed away years ago. Even before he'd become Korban's sponsor- the human being legally responsible for any and all of his full moon activities- RJ looked out for both of his roommates. Having a sponsor, or "handler" as they were sometimes called was just one of the many laws that had been rushed through after the initial outbreak to make sure things did not get out of control. It also kept many of those who weren't able to control themselves in quarantine, a place that still gave Korban nightmares. He was one of the lucky ones who had someone who had applied and succeeded in becoming his sponsor, only having spent nine miserable months in the facility where he'd woken up in after he'd been viciously attacked. RJ took his role very seriously as he did in many things, and Korban was grateful to have someone willing to put everything on the line for him. "Good morning Korban," RJ glances up from his paper, the morning sun giving his ebony skin a warm, chocolate colored tone.

"Morning RJ," he greeted in return, then sat down and huddled around his coffee first, despite his stomach's rumbling protest. The smell of coffee reminded him he was still very human, and no longer the beast he was the night before. He savored his first hot sip then finally indulged in his breakfast.

He caught the worried look in RJ's dark brown eyes and froze mid-bite. "What?"

As his sponsor RJ was legally responsible for everything Korban did, though he was an adult and by all rights should have that control himself. The law was the law, however, and Korban did his best to follow the rules especially because now both his and RJ's freedom depended on it. Violating the law as a werewolf now meant returning to quarantine or death, and those who risked sponsoring the furry by moonlight could also face punishment if the one they sponsored got out of hand. There was even a case of one sponsor serving a life sentence for first degree murder, because the werewolf they sponsored got loose during a full moon and attacked a hiker out for an ill-timed stroll. Even though the werewolf was struck down with a silver bullet, someone had to pay in light of the new, strict laws. The sponsor hadn't even been in the area the night of the assault, and the judgement caused a ripple effect which made others rethink if they were willing to risk sponsoring even their own relatives. He was extremely grateful for RJ acting as his sponsor, something that his good friend didn't have to but was willing to in order to give him even a small chance at a normal life. "Are you okay?" RJ asked after studying him closely for a moment. "You kind of cut it close getting in last night. That's not like you."

"Yeah..." Korban nodded, studying his fork closely and feeling guilty that he'd been so careless to lose track of time, especially at risk of causing RJ trouble. "The interview ran a bit later than I thought it would, and I missed the bus."

His friend smiled hopefully, despite what could have been a bad situation. "How did it go?"

Korban stabbed a piece of egg with his fork. "There was no job. It was all some hoax to get me in. The guy didn't want me, he wanted my wolf."

"What?" RJ sputtered, nearly choking on his coffee.

Korban nodded grimly, swallowing another huge fork full of eggs. "He's insane if he thinks I would bite him. I don't even want to be a werewolf to begin with. He doesn't realize how lucky he is to be human, to have the freedom he has." The same freedom he once had. "Usually when I go in for a job interview the receptionist sees my eyes and turns me away, saying something like the position is full. I think I'd almost take that instead of some lunatic expecting me to rip out of my suit and change into a wolf right then and there."

"Now *that* would make an interesting first impression." Alex barged in, wiping his hands with a stained oil rag. "Sounds like you had a bad night, Lobo. Don't worry amigo, tonight will make up for it."

"Tonight?" RJ raised his eyebrow.

"Yeah. I'm taking you two out." Alex grinned. "My treat. Just got my tax return back, thanks to you helping me file it early."

"Should I wear my running shoes?" While Korban was diligent about staying out of trouble, it seemed that more often than not when they were out on the town trouble found Alex- and vice versa.

"Why do you think I only go out looking for trouble?" Alex asked defensively. "Sometimes the cops show up for reasons completely unrelated to me."

"The last time it wasn't your fault was three years ago. I keep track," RJ reached for his briefcase as he stood up, pausing as he set his coffee mug in the kitchen sink. "Actually, I take it back. That was your fault, the guy just missed and punched the woman sitting next to you."

"She's the one who broke his arm!"

"Regardless, with everything going on I hope you'll at least think twice before starting any trouble. I would like to keep my rap sheet clean, and frankly Korban doesn't need any trouble with the police." RJ turned his gaze to Alex as he spoke, then his eyes went back to Korban. "Any interviews scheduled for today?"

He shook his head. More often than not, he left the day after the full moon open to sleep away most of it. His body was sore and he was still exhausted from the night before.

"Get some rest then, and Alex, let him rest. I have to get going, the delinquents that I'm actually getting paid to teach are waiting." RJ smiled though as he said it. Korban already knew better than anyone that no matter what he said, RJ loved his job- teaching science at one of the worst schools in the city.

The coffee had finally kicked in, and as RJ headed out the door Korban called out, "Give 'em a pop quiz for me!"

2: ENCOUNTER

Howl at the Moon had been their choice hangout since the first night they discovered it, and checked it out under Alex's suggestion. It was a medium sized bar with a nice blend of entertainment to keep busy- some nights live music, other nights karaoke which when they were drunk enough, the three friends would participate in. "Hungry Like the Wolf" was one of the crowd favorites.

They had staked out their usual table in a dark corner. "So, what are we drowning our sorrows in tonight?" Alex scanned the crowd. "The usual drink, or do I go score a lady friend for you?"

Korban mulled that over for a minute. "Drinks first." There wasn't anyone that appealing out on the dance floor. "But I'll get it myself. Either of you want anything?"

"No thanks. I plan on spending most of the night dragging RJ kicking and screaming onto the dance floor."

"I do not kick or scream."

"I'm not even going to dignify that with a response." Korban headed for the bar. Sitting on one of the stools was a blonde woman who did catch his attention. He studies her as he approached the bar, getting closer to a wonderful scent that wasn't perfume, but something more natural and even more attractive. She smelled of vanilla and mint, and something... alluring, but undefined.

This place had its share of working class fakes, but something told him those diamond stud earrings were the real deal. She wore a green silk dress, a classy mid-length that revealed her smooth, long legs and was tight and loose in all the right places. Her long blonde hair was thick and wavy, falling down her back and over her slender shoulders. "What's a nice girl like you doing in a place like this?"

"Do you know how many times I've heard that tonight?" she asked as she stared down at her drink.

"Knowing the regulars here, plus the chances of a woman like you showing up in a hole like this, I'd say enough times that you're fantasizing about me wearing your drink."

The woman turned and stared at him for a moment, then smiled and took a sip of her drink. "That's about right."

"Does it get me your name?"

"I wouldn't push your luck that far."

"Can I at least sit down?"

"It's a free country. For the most part," His stomach fluttered as pretty sky blue eyes met his. He watched as her eyebrows suddenly rose in surprise, "Werewolf!"

He took a step back. "I know, I know. Get away before you call the cops, right?"

"No." She spoke quickly, grabbing his arm. She gave him an embarrassed smile. "I've never met a werewolf before."

"I'm not a science experiment, lady." He was already having

thoughts of returning to the table and keeping in the shadows for the rest of the night. No matter how gorgeous she was, he wasn't sure he had the patience of dealing with any more werewolf fanatics.

"Wait, please. I'm sorry. I didn't mean to insult you." He relaxed at her apology and her brow creased with understanding. "You look like you've had the same kind of day I did."

"You have no idea." He sank on the barstool beside her with a heavy sigh.

"I think I do." Something in her eyes made Korban believe her.

The bartender, a nice college kid named Michael, wandered over. He greeted them with a wide smile, dark blond hair slicked up into spikes that would have seemed messy but had that deliberate curl to them. His brown eyes filled with a friendly warmth that was more than welcome compared to the looks most strangers gave him these days. "Korban, my friend, what can I get you tonight?"

"The usual, Mikey. No ice tonight." His usual was a gin and tonic, the forest-like scent of the liquor usually giving some small amount of comfort to his wolf side.

"And anything for the lady?"

The blonde looked at her near empty glass. "Better get me a refill on my mojito. I may have to throw it at him later."

Korban gave her a toothy grin.

As Mikey returned with their drinks, and the woman spoke again. "So, what brought you here tonight?"

"No fair. I asked first."

She stared into her glass, as if the answer was at the bottom of it. "He's cheating on me."

"Oh." Great. She was on the rebound. "So, are you here for revenge, or…"

"Or to pickle myself until I forget all about it? I'm not sure yet." She flashed him a sad smile. "Your turn."

"No one wants to hire a werewolf. Hell, McDonald's turned me down last week. And yesterday some nut job wanted me to bite him. Like it's so wonderful to be cursed like this."

"That's awful! I'm sorry."

He shrugged nonchalantly. "Nothing anyone can do until they get everything under control. I just do my best to obey their rules and hope that it all passes over, and things can go back to as normal as possible for me."

"I've never really thought about it much before, but they give you a bunch of restrictions, don't they?" She was a stranger to the list, and it was no wonder. He knew you didn't know the list unless it became the guidelines for your survival.

"Yeah. Nothing I can't manage most of the month, really. Just one night a month I turn-"

"Lobo! You're up next Lobo, come on up!" The deejay announces and Korban blinks in confusion, having forgotten if he even put a song in yet or not. He glances over to where Alex and RJ were sitting only to see the mechanic grinning from ear to ear as he flashes him a thumbs up.

His blonde companion sips her drink, gazing at him with an expectant look. No time to chicken out now. He winks to his new friend. "Save my seat?"

She nods, offering a small smile. "I wouldn't dream of giving it away now."

That makes his own smile widen and his heart speed up, heading for the small stage and accepting the microphone from the deejay. "Thanks, Jimmy." The karaoke emcee simply nods, and then the familiar opening beat for Billy Joel's "Uptown Girl" begins to play. Korban shoots a sharp glare over in Alex's direction, but then he sees a smile curve her lips and she raises her glass. He raises his microphone back to her, then sings along with the words on screen. Words he didn't need if truth be told, having this song memorized as one of the ones that used to echo in Cyrus Autos when Alex's grandfather had owned the place.

But staring at the words kept him from fantasizing about murdering his grinning roommate, or from nervously glancing over to his own uptown girl. If anything the amused smirk grew on her lips as she sipped her mojito and watched him as he finished, flipping off Alex as he laughed at his own joke from the table and strode from the stage back over to his lovely, mysterious lady friend.

She raises an eyebrow as he approaches, and he blurts out, "I swear to you, I did not put that song in."

She laughs for the first time, the sound pure joy and unexpectedly delightful, sending a small thrill through him despite himself. "Wow! I didn't know you could sing."

"I am a man, er, werewolf of many hidden talents," he jokes with a flirty wink and she laughs again, making him want to evoke that sound again and again from her. "It's one of the plus sides of being cursed, I suppose, having keener senses means having better pitch, though when someone gets up there and is off key and can be a bit-" Before Korban can finish a huge, bulky man emerged from the crowd and strides over alongside them at the bar.

Shades covered his eyes, even in the darkness of the club. The stranger stood there and flexed his muscles under his straining dark blazer. Even his military-grade buzz cut screamed bodyguard.

"Ma'am, you need to come with me. Your husband just called and he wants you home to talk."

"Hu-husband?" What had he gotten himself into this time?

The woman refused to budge and gave the man a dirty look. "Whatever he's paying you, I'll double it if you go back and tell him to go to hell and come and get me himself."

He actually seems to consider it.

"You didn't say you were *married*!" Korban blurted.

"Unfortunately, I am. For now." She downed the rest of her drink in one gulp.

"Lady, it's not about the money. If it was, I'd be happy to, but I've got orders," he reached for her arm. "Come on, let's go."

Korban suddenly didn't care that the lady was married. He wouldn't stand by while this rude prick bullied the best company he'd had in a while. "If she doesn't want to go, she doesn't have to go." He gave a very convincing growl, knocking back the jerk's hand and putting himself in front of her in one fluid motion. He didn't care that this man looked capable of bench pressing a small car.

"Look, pal, I have to take her with me. Do you know what my boss would do to me if I came back without her?" The looming bully took off his sunglasses and stared him down. His eyes go round suddenly, and Korban feels a surge of satisfaction as the hulking man nervously mutters, "Werewolf..."

"I don't remember saying that I cared." Korban blurts, squaring his jaw as he ignored the man's comment.

"I can't believe Lucas sent one of his goon squad to get me." The blonde shook her head and rubbed her temples, as if a headache was coming on.

"This is a bad side of town, and it's my job to protect you as well as your husband from things like this," he grabs her arm and pulls her to her feet. "We gotta go. Now."

She scowls and tries to yank her arm away. Korban lunges and grabs the man by his collar, giving a low sounding growl and a dangerous look as he demands again, "Let her go. You tell your boss to take it up with me if he doesn't like it."

The bodyguard frowns, and though sweat beads along the man's forehead and he reeks of fear his tone suggests that he wasn't afraid. "Wolf, you're bringing a hell of a lot of trouble down on yourself for some rich bitch who normally wouldn't give you the time of day."

With a snarl, Korban launched a fist at the man's face.

The man must have been used to being hit because he stumbles back, but doesn't fall. "Pretty strong for a puppy." He licked the trickle of dark blood from the corner of his mouth as the crowd spread into a circle around them and began to egg them on.

Alex and RJ nearly ran over a few people rushing to the bar. RJ used his best no-nonsense-teacher-voice as he approached. "What the *hell* is going on?"

"This asshole wanted a snack, so I fed him a knuckle sandwich."

Alex grinned proudly, and RJ frowned and elbowed him in the ribs. "Don't encourage him."

The man charges angrily towards Korban, fist drawn back and then sailing towards his head. Korban braces himself to retaliate and fight back, but never got the chance. An ear-splitting whistle pierces the air, causing him to suddenly curl into himself and clap his hands over his ears in pain. "*Ahhhhhhh!*" Korban grit his teeth as the bodyguard's punch sails past where his head was only seconds ago.

The bodyguard grunts in frustration and moves to bring his knee up to Korban's face but Alex quickly intervenes, yanking his friend back as RJ steps forward, his disapproving look growing sterner by the moment and the dog whistle swinging from his neck. Michael rushes over, yelling, "Hey! Take it outside, no fighting in the bar, or I'm calling the cops!"

"Please, wait!" The woman pleads, her face flushed in embarrassment. "I'll go, this is my fault anyway. I don't want to cause you any more trouble." She glances to Korban and his heart does a little flip-flop when he realizes that statement was directed at him, not Michael.

"Sorry for the disturbance, Mikey," Alex says, shoving a handful of bills onto the bar and pulling Korban in the direction of the exit. "We'll be heading out too."

Michael nodded, looking relieved. The bodyguard paused to glare at Korban as he slips on his dark shades. "I was only trying to do my job. You're lucky this time pup."

Korban averted his gaze momentarily as a fresh swell of anger threatened to let slip another punch into the jerk's jaw. "Next time, make sure your boss knows that Korban Diego sticks up for his friends."

RJ was pretty easy going, but once he got angry, it was best to be on guard. He smacked Korban on the back of the head, which did not help the pounding in his skull. "What the hell were you thinking getting into a pissing contest with some thug? It's not like we have an army! We've only got a werewolf and a mechanic!"

Korban rubbed the back of his head. "Ow, ow. I'm sorry." He straightened his clothes. "But it's not like I could let that lackey bully around... Hey, what is your name?"

Alex started snickering. "You risked your life for some woman whose name you don't even know? Lobo, amigo, you really need to get out more."

"I know, I know-" He spotted her heading for the door. "Hey! Wait up!"

She stopped, and waited for him to catch up. The bodyguard holds the door open and gives a look that Korban chooses to ignore. "Look, I appreciate what you did, but I don't want you and your friends getting hurt so I'm just going to go home, on my own terms. It's better that way." Her eyes were so beautiful it broke his heart to see them so sad. "Thank you, though, Korban. No one's put their self on the line for me in a long time."

"Don't I even get to know your name?"

"I suppose it's the least I could do." She smiled and extended her hand, giving his a firm handshake. "My name is Sophie. Sophie Bane."

"B... B... Bane?!" He's spent the evening flirting with Lucas Bane's wife? The most wealthy and powerful man in the entire city, possibly the country? As he contemplated the various ways the man could ruin his life, Sophie slipped away, outside to where her car was waiting. "Bane?"

As the dark car headed up the street, Alex and RJ emerged from the building. By the look on Alex's face, Korban already knew he'd overheard every word.

"Sophie Bane! You were hitting on the richest woman in the city!" Alex grinned widely. "I can't believe your luck! I can see the headlines in tomorrow's newspapers already. 'Wolfman Rescues Heiress'. I gotta hand it to you, Lobo. That was worth risking our lives for. Talk about friends in high places!" Even RJ couldn't help but smile.

"I wish I could share your enthusiasm, but it turns out the first woman to catch my eye in a while is not only married, but way, way, *way* out of my league."

"Maybe it was fate that you met her. Maybe you'll meet again. After all, didn't you tell me she said she was there to get away from her husband?"

RJ rolled his eyes. "Alex, the unrepentant romantic."

Alex just shrugged. "Anything is possible."

"No, what's possible is Lucas Bane coming down here with the cavalry and beating us all within an inch of our lives."

It was Alex's turn to roll his eyes. "Trust me, Lobo. Everything happens for a reason."

"Whatever you say, Alex." It was hard to believe that after all he'd been through.

"Regardless," RJ interjected, before Alex could go on about it, "it's late, and we almost had a run in with the authorities. I think it may be time to head home before the real cops show up."

The three friends headed home to the garage. Korban closed his eyes and for a split second he catches another whiff of her lingering mint and vanilla scent.

3: AFTER

The morning news revealed nothing about his encounter with the lovely Mrs. Bane last night. He was sort of disappointed because he had secretly hoped for an undercover reporter or some random blogger to have caught a snapshot of him with Sophie, but there was nothing on social media or in the newspaper.

Alex peered over his shoulder as he flipped through the rather thick local section of the paper. He grinned mischievously. "Looking for your Lady Love?"

"Shut up, Alex." Korban sighed and put the newspaper down on the coffee table. "I was looking for the comics."

"Sure you were." Alex taunted, his grin widening.

"If you dish it out, Alex you're on your own," RJ's voice came from the tiny kitchen.

"I'll grab the mail." Korban needed an excuse to get away before he started blushing.

"Hold the fire. I've already grabbed it." Alex beamed, and held up the stack of bills and junk mail proudly. "Though you know, it's a wee bit early for her to send you love letters."

Before Korban could reply, RJ walked over balancing three plates piled high with scrambled eggs, bacon, and sausage. RJ was an excellent cook, which was a good thing because between Korban and Alex the two of them would have starved, poisoned themselves, or burnt down the entire garage with their cooking skills.

Alex started shoveling food into his mouth and RJ smiled, murmuring to Korban as he handed his plate, "That's one way to shut him up."

Korban couldn't help but grin at that. "You've always been the smartest guy I've ever known, RJ."

"It's not about being the smartest," RJ sat down and took a long sip of his coffee. "It's just being smarter than the two of you."

"Hey!" Alex exclaimed after swallowing.

RJ only smiled, and Korban remembered how even though RJ had been the "good boy" he still had a streak of mischief in him. "I knew there was a reason we hung out with you." Korban smiled, flipping through the paper for the classified section. Perhaps today's job search would prove fruitful. After all, last night he had run into the most beautiful heiress in the city. He was feeling lucky for once.

~*~

Sophie woke up stiff on the couch, for a moment disoriented. How she'd gotten there suddenly came to her in a rush of memories. Rushing out and driving until she got lost in the city. Finding a bar and going in, only to have many men try to pick her up, and then the werewolf she'd met who surprised her, protected her from the man sent by Lucas to take her home. Korban... Korban Diego was his name. She remembered his intense, unique golden eyes more than anything. The way his look went dangerous when the bodyguard had grabbed her.

"Good morning," she nearly jumped out of her skin when her husband's voice jolted her from her thoughts. Whirling around, she caught his carefully neutral expression, holding a steaming coffee mug in each hand. "Sleep well, I hope?"

She tried to answer him just as carefully. "Yes actually, I did."

Lucas extended a hand, offering one of the mugs. "Your favorite."

"Thank you." Sophie reluctantly accepted the mug, bringing it close to inhale the scent, and knew instantly that the tea was just how she liked it- mint tea with a pinch of sugar and cream. She sipped it delicately, her gaze meeting his again.

"I think we should talk." Lucas began.

"Isn't that what we are doing now?" Sophie watched as he sat down alongside her on the couch.

"About last night," he interjected, pausing to sip his own tea, or cleverly waiting to see if she'd fill him in without further questioning.

She sighed, holding the mug in both hands. It felt ridiculous having to explain herself to Lucas, when she strongly suspected he was the one cheating on her. "I needed to get away for a little while."

"Sweetheart, if you wanted to get away, why didn't you tell me? We could always go down to the islands for a weekend. I can arrange for a private jet and we can get away from it all, just the two of us if you wanted. I'm sure Daniel could stay with your mother, she always loves a chance to spend time with her grandson."

"No, it's not that. I just wanted to get out for the night." She hated herself for becoming so submissive towards him yet again. Still, he knew just how to push her buttons. If he wasn't able to charm her, he knew bringing up Daniel would always do it. She was mad as hell with Lucas, but wanted to keep it together for her son. "I had a few drinks, met some interesting people," she lowered her gaze to the mug in her hands, watching the ripples move against the ceramic sides, trapped just as much as she was. Looking back up, she studies his expression as she spoke again. "I sat with a werewolf, and one of your men approached me. He said that you sent him there to bring me home."

Lucas flashed a cool smile. "Of course, Sophie. That is a bad area of town. I wouldn't want to risk losing you to any sort of creature that roams that area, human or not." He couldn't hide the suspicion in his eyes when he asked, "So what did this werewolf want?"

"He didn't want anything, just some company at the bar. He was a nice man." A bit flirty, with a sense of humor, and intense, primal eyes... but she'd leave that out. She thought about what he said, and felt sorry that while she was here enjoying a steaming mug of real tea in her condo, this werewolf- no, this man- who had put himself on the line for her sake... he was probably starting his day looking in dumpsters for his breakfast. Then it hit her. Perhaps there was a way she could repay Korban Diego for his kindness. "Lucas... do you know of any job openings at your building?"

"Openings?" Lucas frowned in confusion at the change in subject. "You looking for something to do, Sweetheart?"

"No, no, no... not for me. For..." She gazed down at her breakfast. "For a friend."

"Your werewolf 'friend'?" His voice raised in accusation and he had no right.

She bit back her anger, and ended up snapping at him. "Yes, and so what? He didn't do anything but step in and stand up for me when you sent some muscle to drag me home!" Okay, so she had passed the point of snapping. But for him to accuse her of cheating when he was... it made her boil inside.

"Sophie," his voice was calm and dangerous, "now is not the time to let your temper-"

"Lucas, just stop!" She interjected, eyes narrowing. "Just stop. You have no right to accuse me of anything when you're the one who-"

"Morning Mommy, morning Daddy!" Daniel calls out from the hall, and Sophie dropped the argument like a hot potato.

Lucas was frowning, but he didn't say another word. He broke into a smile as their young son bounded into view, emerging into the living room with a wide grin on his face. His bright blue eyes were sparkling with adoration for both of his parents, and with the enthusiastic morning energy that a young boy naturally had before the expectations of the world wore him down.

Without a word, their argument had mutually ended. For now.

~*~

In the days that followed Korban tried to forget about Sophie. Just when he was involved with his never-ending job hunt and seemingly would forget her; he'd catch a glimpse of a woman with blonde hair or smell vanilla and mint. He felt silly to be crushing on a married woman, but something about her stayed with him. Perhaps because she was the first woman to not flee the moment she caught a glimpse of his unusual yellow eyes, the permanent reminder of his condition. It was inconvenient and very damning in more ways than one, and he often wore sunglasses when out in public.

And while his crush on Sophie seemed to remain, he couldn't help but entertain the possibility that maybe he could have a chance, even if it was a small one. Her husband *was* cheating. So perhaps Alex was right and maybe he did have a chance encounter with her for a reason.

Then he would think about it and worry that he was obsessing, or perhaps in some twisted way stalking her. Not in the traditional follow the object of your affections and watch their every move, but trying to catch a glimpse of her in the papers or online, hoping for a chance to run into her again when he was out. For the past week now, he'd made a nightly journey over to Howl at the Moon, just in case she'd show up.

Michael raised his eyebrows when he glanced up from wiping the bar down one night when Korban wandered in. "Hey Korban! What is this, the eighth day in a row? Must be having a rough month." He poured him a tall beer from the tap and slid it across the smooth wooden surface.

Korban offered him a small smirk then glanced around. The bar was pretty empty tonight and there was no sign of Sophie, to his obvious displeasure. He sighed and took a long swig of beer. His metabolism was super-fast and it would take more than a few mugs of beer to get him remotely buzzed. " Yeah, no one is hiring. I can help Alex out at the garage, but that's more his thing. I'd rather do something I'm good at."

Michael idly dried a glass. "Well, what type of work are you looking to do?"

Korban stared at the remaining ring of froth that floated on the top of his beer. He gave a sad smirk. "You know what's funny? I honestly have no idea. I just hope that something will turn up that I'll be good at. Maybe even something that I'll like doing. I want to get on with my life again. I don't want to worry about mooching off my friends to live. I want to make it on my own. I just hope that I strike lucky and find something I love doing in the process. Right now I'd take anything and just hope that I'll be happy with it, for now."

Michael nodded. "I know what you mean. I was going to college on a basketball scholarship, but freshman year I shattered my ankle and suddenly I wasn't sure what I wanted to do. I'm just now getting my act together. I switched majors and I'm going into psychology of all things." He paused, setting the clean glasses on the shelves behind him. "It'll happen for you too, Korban. One day it will just click and you'll know what you want to do. It may seem right now that it's hopeless. The chips may be stacked against you in particular because of the world at large right now, but I know you'll get it together soon enough." He offered an encouraging smile. "Tell you what. That one's on me. Consider it a start to your luck turning around."

Korban blushed and went for his wallet, "Really? It's okay Mikey-"

Michael shook his head. "Really," he raised his bottle of water to Korban's glass. "A toast to turning our luck around."

"I'll toast to that," Korban clinked the glass, then finished the rest in one swig. Just like coffee, there was something about having a beer that made him feel more human. His eyes glistened when Michael finished off his bottle of water. "You know what Mikey? You really are going to make a great psychologist someday."

~*~

Even with the commotion of Hancock Airport, the murmur of the crowd and the booming rush of jet engines landing and taking off, Sophie knew that before she could even spot her younger sister she would hear her. So when she heard the familiar cry, "Sissy!" she turned and smiled.

The petite blonde nearly stumbled in her vivid pink high heels as she waved and was thrown off balance by her luggage. She turned heads where ever she went but was especially out of place amidst the commuters and travelers with her short, bright red designer dress and matching bags.

"Nikki!" Sophie rushed over to her younger sister, who grabbed her into a bag-filled hug. "How was your flight?"

"Not too bad for a commercial jet, but hey, it made a few of the passenger's day. Except for Mr. Twenty-one B, whose wife is probably making him sleep on the couch the next couple nights," she laughed.

Sophie remembered her own recent experience passing out on the couch and blushed in memory. Nikki prattled on as the driver took her bags and put them into the trunk of the limousine.

"It's good to have you home. How was your trip?" Sophie asked as they sat in the back seat.

"Manhattan was wonderful, even though the photographer worked me nearly to death. But the shots he got! Wait until you see them. Probably my best work yet, and I was already offered another job for Victoria's Secret's next catalog, maybe even some advertisements with them." Nikki beamed. "It's so exciting! You know, you'd probably make a great model if you wanted, Sissy. I could talk to my agent, get you in a couple shoots with me if you'd like."

Sophie shook her head and laughed as the limo pulled away from the curb, "Thanks, but no thanks. You know I'm terribly camera shy." She made a point to keep a low profile because of this, as well as to give her son a chance at a semi-normal life. Lucas was the one who loved the spotlight, it was good for business.

"Well, if you ever change your mind, you know who to call." Nikki glanced up to make sure that the partition was closed and the driver was focused on the road. "Did you confront Lucas yet?"

Sophie looked down, shaking her head, "No," she sighed, staring out the window, watching the highway roll past. "I don't know how to ask him about it."

Nikki clicked her tongue in disapproval. "You found another woman's underwear in the laundry. I'd say that's evidence enough he's been fooling around on you."

"I know, and maybe I'm procrastinating on talking to him about it. I just... I don't know." Sophie trembled and wrapped her arms around herself, feeling suddenly cold despite the unusually warm spring day.

"Sissy, I know you still love him. But if he's going behind your back and cheating on you, you need to stand up for yourself. I know you're worried about what will happen, especially with Daniel, but I'm worried about what this is doing to you. The longer you stay in this unhappy marriage... I just don't want to see you end up miserable because of it all."

Sophie shook her head. "I'll talk to him, when the time is right."

Nikki sighed, rolling her eyes dramatically, "Are you *sure* you don't want me to talk to him? I'd be more than happy to give him a piece of my mind."

Sophie shot her a look of warning. "Please *don't* Nikki!"

"I only wish you'd have that same temper with him," Nikki chided.

"Believe me," Sophie's gaze turned somber, "I do too."

4: INVITATION

Crescent moons were his favorite. Half moons made him feel the wolf pacing, waiting to break free. New moons made him feel strangely empty inside. And full moons... that went without saying.

Tonight they ate pizza under the starlight, watching the city glistening in the not-too-far-off distance and the large crescent moon hanging heavy in the sky. On clear nights they would sit on the top of Cyrus Autos and RJ would barbeque and they'd laugh and drink a few beers.

Sitting in a row, the three friends dangled their feet over the edge of the building and discussed everything and nothing at all.

"So how'd it go today, Lobo?" Alex asked, handing him an ice cold bottle of beer from the cooler.

"Not too bad." He was in a good mood for some reason. Maybe it was the beer and pizza. Or maybe it was the moon. "All rejections, but I got to eight interviews. A record in one day, even for me."

RJ smiled. "I admire your perseverance, Korban."

"More like stubbornness." Korban grinned, taking a swig of beer.

Alex snickered. "Ain't that the truth."

Korban laughed. "So, what about you two?"

"I'm drinking this one for the kids," RJ lifted his bottle to the stars. "They've finished their state exams, so now the real learning can begin."

"That's great man. You've always had a way with kids," Alex grinned as he lifted his bottle to RJ's. "To the kids."

Their bottles clinked together and the three friends enjoyed a long swig.

Alex gazed up at the moon. "I did pretty well today too. A half dozen or so oil changes, two tune ups, and a brake job. Enough to pay the power, water, and some to spare on this case of beer."

They tipped their bottles to the moon again. "To the garage."

After nearly finishing their beers on the second toast, RJ and Alex turned to Korban. Alex's dark brown eyes glistened with delight. "How about a toast for chance meetings?"

Korban turned and stared toward something distant and unseen over the skyline. "I don't know. I mean, it was just a lucky break Alex. I'll probably never see her again, and she's probably forgotten all about me by now."

Alex shook his head. "I don't think so."

"You did defend her from that thug," RJ added helpfully. "Chances are she remembers you Korban."

"Maybe," Korban smirked. "Seems like Alex here is rubbing off on you too RJ."

RJ smiled. "As long as he doesn't rub off too much I'll be okay. My students would never let me live it down if I was called to the principal's office as much as you two were."

Alex laughed, raising his bottle again and grinning at Korban. When RJ tipped his bottle up in turn it was too much. Chuckling he joined the toast. "Fine, fine. To Sophie."

"And to fate," Alex added before they finished off their beers.

~*~

The more things changed, the more they really did stay the same. Korban couldn't help but think the phrase as he sat on the wooden bench beside RJ as they waited to meet with Sergeant McKinnon. The courthouse still had the usual suspects; lawyers rushing about in expensive suits with Styrofoam cups of coffee in hand, police officers meandering through the hallways with suspects in handcuffs, the dull chatter ringing through the air. He'd been here at least once a month since he was released from quarantine and even the ones in handcuffs seemed familiar. There were slight differences, like the lingering scent of another one like him from a previous appointment on the bench, the stink of wolf adding to his anxiety. RJ would glance his way when he tensed, asking without words if he was going to be okay. He always breathed in the familiar scent of his friend, his brother, his savior, and he would nod. *Get a grip, Korban.*

RJ didn't have to do this. He could easily have washed his hands of him five years ago. Korban could have been left in the psychiatric rehabilitation facility, locked away and left to the needles that poked and prodded him, the strange chemical smells and cold, studious eyes of the ones who ran the facility...

One of the suspects walking past leapt back, catching a glimpse of Korban's gold eyes. The hardened criminal turned frantic, trying to dart up the hall. The cops held him and gruffly commanded him to calm down as he struggled to escape. The man began to cry and confess to everything he'd ever done, just as long as they put him somewhere far away from the monster.

RJ put a hand on his shoulder, which kept him in his seat. A wave of emotion coursed through him, from numbing shock to fiery rage, to a deep ache. Thankfully as he adjusted his shades the man's pleas faded into the distance and the door opened. Finally another friendly face appeared.

At first glance Sergeant Tim McKinnon was warm and welcoming. He was a couple inches shorter than Korban and his build slightly heavier than average, a well-earned beer belly beginning to bulge around his middle. Tim's well-trimmed beard framed his face in light brown hair, flecks of silver beginning to emerge here and there along his jaw. "Korban, RJ, come on in," Tim waves them into his office.

Breathing a sigh of relief, the pair step into the small office. There were several small clay pots with tiny pine trees in them, giving the room a wild, clean scent. The rest of the room was an organized mess- a desk with stacks of unfiled papers, walls lined with bookshelves teeming with books on law and the occult, and a single corkboard by the door which had a bunch of children's drawings hanging on it. They sat in worn but comfortable old leather office chairs and gathered around the cluttered desk. "Sorry about the hold up, Donna was going on about seein' some supermodel at the airport yesterday," Tim shrugged casually and miraculously pulled a paper folder from the clutter on his desk with Korban's name on the tab. He opens it up and plucks a pen from the coffee mug that proclaimed "World's Greatest Dad". His pale blue eyes glinted with a friendly warmth that lingered when he spoke about his wife, but slid to shrewd, neutral cop eyes when bringing up the business at hand. Tim, like Michael, didn't give Korban a frightened or odd look as he sat across from him. "So, another month down, and no incidents to report?"

RJ shakes his head. "No, the change happened, he was locked in the garage in time and the only casualty was one of the hubcaps that Alex forgot to put up."

"How is Alex these days? Haven't seen his name on any incident reports lately," Tim grins, scribbling down some notes.

"He's been behaving himself," RJ smirks and Korban echoes the smile.

"Miracle of miracles," Tim chuckles, then continues down the list. "Any luck on the job hunt, Korban?"

He shakes his head, sobering a little. Though his eyes widen suddenly, lighting up as a memory resurfaces. "One guy I interviewed with, he offered me money to-" His stomach churns again, sick at the thought. "To bite him."

Tim's hand pauses, hovering over the paper. His jaw drops open and then suddenly he drops the pen and it rolls to the floor. He raises an eyebrow as he stares at Korban incredulously. "What? Really?" He scrambles for his fallen pen, then pulls out a small stack of yellow post-its. "What day did this occur? Who was this interview with? Who asked you this?"

Korban blushes. "It was the night of the full moon, an interview with the hiring manager at Crucible, the steel foundry… guy's name is Brett Kensington." He could still see his shiny name placard on his desk.

Tim's frown grows as he jots the name down. "Thanks for telling me this. I'll have to look in on him, make sure he's not biting off more than he can chew." He flashes Korban a smile, which Korban returns in favor. It vanishes when Tim asks, "How much did you turn down?"

"One hundred grand, and that was just the start," Korban winces, remembering the tempting check sliding across the desk.

"I think I will be sure to pay him a visit then," Tim leans back in his chair with a frown. "One hundred thousand dollars… that'd be enough for many to do it. Why didn't you?"

"Because of-" Korban began, but what was the real reason he turned down such an offer? Sure he could have used that money. But he knew the risks. "Because even if it wasn't illegal, even if my life wasn't on the line… I wouldn't wish this on my worst enemy."

~*~

One morning after breakfast a week later Korban and Alex were working downstairs in the garage. RJ had already headed out to school and Alex had his hands full so he'd asked if Korban would mind helping him out that day. Having nothing better to do or any interviews lined up for the day, of course he agreed.

To Alex cars were pieces of art. He would stand and admire them then delicately open the hood, and mutter to himself or occasionally whistle at the engine. He knew every nut and bolt and told Korban a thousand of different names of various pieces of metal.

Being around cars wasn't all that exciting to Korban, but watching Alex's face light up as he went to work at his craft was inspiring. Korban longed for a job he could feel this passionate about. It was depressing to think he might never have that. It was hard enough to find any job, never mind one he actually liked doing.

"Earth to Lobo! Hey when you get back down here, amigo, mind passing me that socket wrench, the one with the yellow handle?" Alex peeked out from under the hood.

"Oh. Sorry, bro," Korban shook his head, in attempt to clear his muddled brain. He handed him the wrench.

"Thanks," Alex went back to work under the hood, as delicate and as experienced as a surgeon performing surgery.

Korban watched as Alex loosened one bolt then tightened another, swapping out pieces and putting it all back together. He was impressed when Alex suddenly looked to him and grinned. "Let's see how she's doing," he tossed him the key. "Start her up, Lobo."

"Aye, Captain," Korban grinned then slid into the driver's seat and to start it up. The engine purred to life without any hesitation. It was as if Alex made the car new again. "Wow."

He revved the engine and Alex beamed proudly at his handiwork. "*Beau-ti-ful.* They'll be picking this baby up in a half hour, and we'll have two more oil changes in and out by then," Alex mopped the sweat from his forehead with an oil-stained rag. "You know, it's kind of nice having an extra pair of hands around, Korban. If you wanted I mean, if nothing else comes up. I could use your help around here, ya know?"

Korban looked away, blushing. He felt embarrassed- his friends had done so much for him already that he wouldn't ever ask for anything more from them. Now Alex was offering him a job. Alex maybe looked rough around the edges, but his friends all knew he had a big heart.

"Seriously, bro. I don't mind hanging out with a friend all day, doing what I do best," Alex closed the car hood and wiped it with a clean, wooly cloth.

"Th-thanks, Alex," Korban managed, helping him collect his tools. "I appreciate it, I really do, but-"

Before he could say another word, a sleek black car that probably cost more than any other car in the garage combined pulled in. "Whoa..." Alex's eyes lit up like Christmas had come early this year. "Nice ride."

Korban gave a low whistle of approval. The driver and the passenger stepped out and suddenly the good feeling was gone. Both men were big- in a solid way that only those Mafia thugs in the movies were. Clad like men in black from the shiny black shoes to the sunglasses, they both went around and opened the back door of the car and led over a man that Korban and Alex had only seen on magazines and online articles before.

Alex's jaw dropped open and he was stunned silent. Korban only managed to mutter a few words. "Oh shit."

Lucas Bane, in his tailored suit that cost more than the car they'd just finished repairing, smiled coldly at the two of them in their oil and dirt stained jump suits. "Good afternoon... gentlemen. I am Lucas Bane, head of Bane Corporation. Is there a Mr. Korban Diego here?"

Lucas radiated arrogance, and something in his strained politeness grated against Korban's nerves. If he wasn't so scared on what those two thugs were capable of doing to him, he'd have shot his mouth off. And RJ thought he had no control. Swallowing the lump that had suddenly appeared in his throat, Korban managed to get out, "That's me."

Lucas turned up his cocky smile. Even when he smiled his eyes remained cold and calculated. "It's a pleasure to meet you, Mr. Diego."

One of his thugs cracked his knuckles and Alex paled. Korban tensed, but kept his own fear at bay. Fear made him stupid and that was the last thing they needed at that moment. So, as much as he hated it, he ignored this pompous prick's attempt to shovel shit in his face. "The pleasure is all mine, Mr. Bane."

"Please, call me Lucas."

All right, he'd had it with the formal exchange of niceties. "How may I help you, Lucas?"

"Right to the point, I admire that. Perhaps my associate was right about you after all, Mr. Diego. I've heard great things about you." Lucas walked over to them, thugs in tow. He studied Korban for a long, tense moment, an unspoken challenge reflected in those cold eyes. "So it is true. You are a werewolf."

"Look, Lucas, if this is about your wife, nothing happened, okay? I just don't like some bully roughing up a lady, so I stepped in, but-" He stopped because the look in Lucas's eyes was clearly one of surprise- perhaps he was there on different business? But what?

Korban sighed, "Look, Lucas, if I can do something to help you, let me know. But if you've just come down here to see the big bad wolf then I suggest you come another day 'cause I'm not in the mood for it right now, okay?"

Lucas feigned an innocent smile. "I must say, Mr. Diego, I do appreciate your, ahh, honesty as well. Thank you for looking after my wife the other night. You see, I believe that what goes around comes around. I've heard that you are looking for a job and I think I have a position available. Especially since you've come so highly recommended to me."

Korban exchanged a glance with Alex, who despite his paleness managed a small smile. Had Sophie just hooked him up with a job? "Who...?"

Lucas only smiled and said, "Let us just say you now have friends in very high places, Mr. Diego."

He couldn't hide his grin. Perhaps she hadn't forgotten about him after all.

"I'm afraid I only have a start-up position available right now, but I'll see to it personally that you are well taken care of and if you come as qualified as our friend says then I'm sure you will advance quickly. Though, there is another matter of course," Lucas paused.

Korban knew by the look in the man's eyes there was a catch. "Which matter?"

"As you know, right now there are quite a few people out there who are… uncomfortable around those with lycanthropy. I think it would be best for you as well as my employees if you meet everyone first, give them a chance to warm up to the idea of having you around. My company is hosting a charity ball, to raise funds for the children's hospital. I would like to personally invite you to attend, as a way to break the ice, so to speak." Lucas reached in his jacket, retrieving an envelope and handing it tentatively to him.

Korban accepted the invitation, then nodded. "I appreciate the invitation. Are you sure it's really necessary though?"

Lucas smiled smoothly. "If I didn't think it was, I wouldn't be here right now, Mr. Diego. I do hope you will accept my offer."

The thought of spending an evening under prying eyes made his stomach churn in anxiety. But on the other hand, the chance to see Sophie again made his heart soar, even if it would be in the presence of her slimy, cheating husband. His future boss. Go figure. "All right, I'm down. Sounds like a party."

"Excellent. Of course you can bring a friend if you'd like," Lucas glanced at his watch, then offered them another plastic smile. "Well, gentlemen, I am afraid that I have a few other appointments to attend to, so I apologize for leaving in a hurry. I just had to meet you and thank you for seeing that my wife safely returned. Good day, Mr. Diego, and...?" He turned to Alex, as if just now noticing him there.

Alex wasn't fazed at all, because he'd spent the last few minutes trying to be invisible. "Alejandro Cyrus. If you ever need any auto services my shop is always open. Well, except on full moon nights."

"Of course, Mr. Cyrus," He quickly shook both their hands. "Thank you again, Mr. Diego. Good day to you gentlemen."

Lucas motioned for his men and they piled back in their fancy car and soon were off, leaving as quickly as they came. As soon as the fancy car vanished down the road, Alex let out a whoop of victory. "All right! You did it!" He grinned, grabbing Korban and pulling him under his arm for an affectionate noogie. "What did I tell you?! Looks like she didn't forget about you after all! Wow!"

Korban laughed and despite himself felt his cheeks burn with mild embarrassment. They headed back into the garage.

"Wow though... that is just amazing Lobo!" Alex grinned, and they began to get back to work again. "Lucas Bane, the richest man in the city, dropping in on us like that! I guess it's good that you didn't put the moves on his wife! Those goons looked like they could crush us with their bare hands."

"You, maybe," Korban teased, "but not the 'big, bad wolf.'"

~*~

When the three-quarter moon rose over the skyline as night fell its pull was strong. Basking on the roof once again in the pale moonlight, the three friends began making preparations for the charity ball which was at the convention center tomorrow night.

"Man, I wish I could go with you guys but I'm swamped. There's no way I'll be able to get free in time. Stupid brake recall," Alex sipped his beer, gazing up longingly at the sky.

"Well, on the bright side, we don't have to force you to wear a penguin suit Alex," RJ joked with a grin. "Remember prom night?"

"Oh please, don't talk about *that* again." Alex sat up, giving his friend a playful jab in the ribs. "Okay, so I spiked the punch and you ended up helping me empty my stomach in the girl's bathroom. How did I know back then that vodka was so strong?"

Korban chuckled. "I'll never forget your fist fight with the deejay before that, because you wanted to sing along with Kurt Cobain."

Alex grinned. "I was lucky that I knocked out the speaker instead of him, huh? That was a bitch to pay off though. Took me six months of allowance. Pops did not make it easy on me either." He sighed, gazing back up at the sky. "Look at us. Business is thriving. Lobo here has a job lined up, and RJ is being paid doing what he does best- keeping delinquents under control."

They laughed together at that. "It's a tough job, but someone has to do it. Might as well be someone with my varied experience."

"You guys have fun tomorrow, but don't forget about me! I'm going to need all the juicy details when you get home tomorrow night. Don't forget a single thing!" Alex made them promise.

"Trust me Alex, I have a feeling tomorrow night will be unforgettable."

5: GALA

No words seemed appropriate to describe the first impression that the ball made on them, but Korban managed to sum it up in a breathless, "*Whoa.*"

Outside of the Oncenter it was the full red carpet treatment, just like in the movies. Spotlights lit up the night sky from the sidewalk as many of the city's elite, including a handful of local celebrities, decorated the scene in the latest fashion. Limousines and other dark, stylish cars pulled up and dropped off famous faces before slipping away into the night. Camera crews lined up along the sidewalk with their sound and lighting equipment, clustered in small bunches here and there to snag whoever they could for a quick interview.

"I hope the money they raise tonight is more than what this party cost," RJ muttered, keeping close to Korban's side.

Korban nodded in agreement and tried desperately not to look too hard for Sophie. He knew the chances of seeing her in such a crowded event and acknowledging him publicly was as likely as his lycanthropy suddenly vanishing. Still, he couldn't help but anticipate running into her again. Though he was certain that if he could focus on it hard enough he could scent her out. The thought colored his cheeks and he continued gazing around to keep RJ from noticing.

They handed their tickets to the bouncer at the convention center's entrance. There were a few second-glances from security when they noticed his eyes but he was on the list so they stepped aside. The night was looking up and Korban nodded to them confidently as they passed clean through the metal detector and followed the crowd through the hall to the ballroom.

Inside was the most glamorous scene he had ever seen; chandeliers glistening above, popular music being played by a live symphony, tables that spanned many yards groaning under the weight of ice sculptures and fancy bite-sized hors d'vors. The smell of this place hit Korban like a buffet of aromas. Expensive perfume, sweat, and all those delicious foods combined into a delightful buffet of scents that he inhaled deeply.

He knew then that the woman he sought out wasn't there. Not yet. Her sweet, unique scent had yet to join this assortment, but when it did he would know. His heart was already fluttering with the excitement of seeing her again that night.

Her mother had always called it "fashionably late", but to Sophie it was always just plain behind schedule. For an event like this, she'd enlisted Nikki to help her with the preparations. As the woman of the evening, she had to look her best. And if there was one thing her little sister knew, it was how to make an entrance.

Her sister was quiet as she brushed Sophie's long silky hair, her lips pursed and eyes unfocused as though deep in thought. Gazing at her younger sister's reflection, Sophie asked, "What's wrong?"

"Oh, it's nothing really. I just have a lot going on, that's all. Big photo shoot for a calendar coming up, and the cover of *Vogue* next week." Nikki's gaze shifted from Sophie's scalp up to her reflection, smiling. "You're going to be the one who knocks 'em dead tonight."

Sophie blushed as she looked down. "I get so nervous in front of crowds, and I've never been patient enough to deal with the photographers at these things. Remember my wedding?"

Nikki smiled. "I'm amazed that you got any decent pictures at all. It was pretty windy that day."

"The photographer had to follow us like a stalker to get the pictures we did, and now he's off in Africa photographing wild life." Sophie laughed, then looked down again. "No, I couldn't model. I'm too camera shy, and I don't really want all that attention. That's more of Lucas's thing. I'm happy just taking care of Danny, being at home and taking care of things there."

"Sophie, the happy home-maker," Nikki teased, playfully fluffing her hair with neatly manicured fingernails. "I guess one of us needed to fill that role."

"Things change, you know? I have my son and husband to think of. I do my best to keep my family together." Her voice cracked a little at the end. "Oh Nikki, I just don't know what to do!" She buried her face into her hands, not caring if she smeared her makeup.

Nikki went to her sister's side, kneeling and putting a comforting arm around her back. "What is it? What's wrong?" She asked worriedly, pulling out tissues from her purse.

"I try so hard to keep it together, and even then it falls apart," Sophie accepts the tissues, dabbing her eyes and then softly blowing her nose. Her eyes narrowed as she composed herself again. "He's cheating on me. I mean, I know I told you this before, but now I know for certain. I overheard him calling someone late the other night, and…" She became too choked up to finish the thought.

Nikki's jaw dropped open. "Oh my gosh! I'm so sorry Sophie… that *asshole*!" She got up to her feet, wielding the brush like a club. "Let me go out there, I'll give him a piece of my mind-"

"No! Please," Sophie's expression softened. She slumped down a little in her chair, searching the floor for the answer. "I'm so confused. I love him, and even if it hurts, I want things to work out. For me and him, and especially for Daniel. Maybe if I talked to him, we could work things out. All we do lately is argue, and the funny thing is I miss him when he's not there. I want this to work, Nikki. I love him, I really do, but lately I can't trust him. I mean, is he working late? Or meeting some whore on the side?"

Nikki abandoned the brush on the vanity and put her hands on her sister's shoulders, gazing again at their reflections. "Listen, sweetie. If Lucas is really cheating on you, you can't trust him. Without trust, you can't truly love someone. It just doesn't work, relationships are built on trust, and once that is gone... I just don't want to see you get hurt, sis." She leaned a little closer to whisper. "You know, there were rumors I heard somewhere that he was seeing another woman, but I didn't want to say anything because I didn't think Lucas could do that to you. Is it true then, too, that you were downtown with a werewolf a couple weeks ago?"

Sophie remembered him then, his darkly handsome features, those startling amber eyes. Korban. He'd stood up for her despite barely knowing her and he'd made her laugh when she wasn't sure she would ever smile again. Even now she smiled, thinking of his toothy grin. "Yes, I met a rather nice man who happens to be a werewolf."

"*Really?*" Nikki grinned. "What was he like? Were you scared? Was he cute?"

"Scared?! No, he didn't scare me," Sophie picked up her brush and continued to stroke her already silky blonde hair, "but he made me laugh. He had a sense of humor. His eyes were amazing. Yellow wolf eyes, but they were vibrant against his tan skin. He had the sort of look that you'd recognize instantly, even in a crowded room."

"Sort of like Lucas, hmm?" Nikki stated more than asked, puffing a small spray of a sweet perfume on her.

"Yes, only different. He was very nice, with a good sense of humor. I was a bit taken aback when I realized what he- what his condition was, but other than that he was a decent guy." She added, as an afterthought, "And by that time of night, trust me, his company was more than welcome."

Nikki studied her sister shrewdly. "So are you going to *thank* him, you know, for being there for you?"

"Of course. I'm thinking of writing him, because I sort of left abruptly-"

"Oh, no, no, no Sophie," Nikki gave a small laugh. "That's not what I meant at all. You said he's a pretty looking puppy, right? Why not use that to your advantage?"

Sophie turned to look her sister in the eye. "What are you getting at, Nikki?" She'd never seen that look in her sister's eyes before.

"What I'm saying is, 'do unto others as other unto you', my dear sister. If Lucas wants his girl on the side, I say you find this... friend of yours and do the same." Nikki grinned. "It's only fair."

She couldn't believe what she was hearing. Staring at her sister in disbelief, Sophie blurted, "You're... you're **not** being serious?!"

Nikki simply shrugged. "It's only a suggestion, Sophie. I just think after all you've done for him, a little vengeance wouldn't hurt."

"No. Absolutely not," Sophie shook her head. "I couldn't do it. I love Lucas, and I would never use someone else like that. It wouldn't help anything, but it would definitely make things worse. I couldn't put Daniel through all that." She quickly changed the subject because her mind could not yet wrap around what her sister suggested. "It's getting late. I'd better go."

"Yeah," Nikki pat her shoulder again, flashing a reassuring smile. "Go knock 'em dead."

Sophie finished reapplying her mascara and gave her sister a hug before leaving. "Thanks."

"Don't mention it. Have fun!"

Sophie rushed out to where Lucas was waiting, adding his much simpler final touches to his own elegant evening wear- smoothing his jacket, checking his cuff links. He smiled and offered her his arm as she approached, "You look beautiful."

Even though her mind was still spinning, his smile still made her knees go weak. Taking his arm she whispered, "Thank you."

Her dress was a simple but elegant design, white shimmering cloth that accented perfectly every curve of her body. She wore a tennis bracelet made of white gold on her right wrist, and a matching necklace with a tiny pendant in the shape of a heart at the end- an anniversary present Lucas bought her after their first year together. Her earrings were simple diamond studs and the only other accessories were her engagement and wedding rings. Her hair was a silky, golden waterfall that trailed down her back.

"Ready?" He asked her softly, more than likely feeling the tension in her arms as he took her arm in his. The familiar gesture gave her some measure of comfort when they were about to face a crowd of strangers.

"Yeah," she smiled at him and knew that for tonight he had her exactly where he wanted her, despite herself.

His kiss on her lips sealed the deal.

~*~

The place was packed and by the time they managed to get close enough to the stage the lights dimmed and the spotlights burst on, bright beams of light directing attention toward the stage. Every television network was broadcasting the event and all eyes turned to where the spotlights came to rest.

"Think they'll do a musical number?" Korban managed to crack between a wide, amused grin.

RJ chuckled. "If they do, pinch me, because then I'm certain this is a dream."

Before Korban could respond an announcer's voice boomed from above. "Ladies and gentlemen, we are proud to welcome you tonight to the annual…" He droned on about the Bane Corporation, the charity raising funds for the children's hospital, thanking the other minor sponsors for the event. There was a thundering applauseand then it went quiet again. Even amidst the crowd, there came the familiar hint of vanilla and mint that he'd been craving since their encounter at the bar. "Without further ado, I present to you our host and highest donor for tonight's fundraiser, Mr. Lucas Bane, CEO of Bane Corporation, and his lovely wife Sophie."

Korban's head jerked toward the direction where the announcer was pointing and realized the announcer had been wrong. Sophie was not simply 'lovely'. She was the most beautiful woman in the room. He could smell mingled with her minty scent that she was nervous, but she managed to hide it quite well behind that dazzling smile.

RJ studied his friend with a slow smile, shaking his head. "You got it bad, Korban. I've never seen you so interested in anyone else before."

He didn't say anything, because he couldn't lie to RJ and didn't know what else to say. Sophie was literally the woman of his dreams, and tragically enough she was attached to the most powerful man in his known universe. Sure, he was cheating on her- Korban wondered who he could possibly consider a better catch than Sophie- but the chances of her being remotely interested in him were at the very least non-existent. It was something he knew but eventually would accept. Contrary to Billy Joel, uptown girls weren't interested in downtown boys. Never mind the big, bad wolf.

Lucas walked over to the microphone and smiled. The two of them together were a portrait of the rich and the famous. Korban wanted to hit him. Why was it that all the assholes in the world got all the best women? "Thank you all for coming tonight. I am honored to be a part of hosting this charity ball in order to make this dream possible for our city."

As if on cue the audience broke into applause. They all loved him; he was the one who made this all possible. What a wonderful man. Oh, how Korban wished to make it all come crashing down on that snake. New boss or not.

"Without further speeches of self-plugging, let's get this party started. Thank you all again for coming tonight!" Lucas dazzled them with a brilliant white grin and a wave, then stepped off the stage. The music kicked in, and someone on stage began singing a song that he'd heard on the radio; but Korban was watching Sophie, following her with his eyes as she made her way through the crowd beside Lucas.

"Go talk to her, you're making me sick with those puppy-dog eyes," RJ gave him a sharp poke in the ribs. "Go on. Now's your chance- he's been snagged by some reporters and she's making a break for the punch table. Go get her, Lobo." He gave him a smack on the shoulder, grinning at Korban with encouragement.

"Ow! Fine, fine- I don't want to be black-and-blue by the time I get over to her." Mustering up his courage, he made his way over to the table covered in various beverages. Someone behind the biggest crystal bowl he'd ever seen used a ladle to pour punch for everyone into real crystal cups. He took a cup when offered one, nodding his head in thanks. He didn't even sip his punch, though- the next thing he knew Sophie Bane was heading right toward him.

~*~

Sophie felt hot under that spotlight, and with every eye on her and her husband she felt a sweat drop slowly glide down her back. The moment Lucas was finished and snagged by reporters, Sophie politely excused herself, darting over to the refreshments table. She needed a drink, something to wet her suddenly cotton-dry mouth. She hated this, all these strangers staring at her with mixed expressions. She should have been used to the attention. Her father had made headlines even before she was born. Still, she could remember passing out on stage during a Christmas pageant when she was twelve. Some things never changed.

Then as if by some miracle she spotted a familiar face. She was so surprised that she instantly headed toward him, as if he was just an illusion mingling in the crowd.

She smiled at him as she grew nearer, relieved to finally have someone who was not a total stranger to talk to. Besides, she still owed him a thank you for the other night.

~*~

His knees went weak under the power of her smile. So many promises hidden in those lovely, curving lips- or maybe he just should have taken Alex's advice and got out more often. All that pent-up innuendo would be the death of him if he did not release it soon.

He just couldn't help it, as much as he tried. Before meeting Sophie all other women seemed to treat him the same. Of course,

Sophie was out of his league and married. Perhaps part of her allure was the fact that having her could be dangerous. A part of him craved danger after all, even though he fought hard against those animalistic urges. He had to play nice, play human- even if the beast beneath his skin dictated otherwise. He returned her smile, swooning inwardly as he inhaled her scent so near to him.

As she stopped to greet him he remembered first laying eyes on her, and suddenly knew what to say.

Offering his cup to her, he grinned. "Good evening. A drink for the lady?" He let his eyes meet hers, "You may need it, in case I don't behave."

She smiled, taking the cup. "Is that a fantasy of yours, Korban? Being hosed down by a woman's drink?"

He grinned, meeting her challenge. "Not just any woman's drink."

Sophie's cheeks flush pink and she sipped the drink, perhaps to do something to hide her blush. "Then you must love flirting with danger, as you already know I'm married."

"Me? Flirt?" He feigned innocence but that grin broke through. "That's a strong accusation, Mrs. Bane."

She laughed, "You are just too much, Korban Diego."

"My teacher used to say that a lot," That laughter never left his eyes, but something just as intense remained there a moment later when they both stopped laughing. "You look beautiful tonight."

The way he said it, with his voice deepening slightly, sent a fine tremor down her spine. This time she couldn't suppress her blush, "Thank you."

There was a moment when neither of them spoke. Sophie

took another sip of her drink, her expression sobering a little as she spoke again, "I owe you more than a thank you, for what you did the other night. Not too many people look out for each other in this city these days."

"I know." She sensed something, catching a pained look as it flashes in his eyes.

She touched his arm, unknowingly sending electricity through his skin, and all through his body. "I wanted to apologize too, for leaving so abruptly. I just didn't want to cause a scene, and I really didn't want to see you get hurt over me."

"You don't have to apologize. He never should have touched you. I can't stand pushy bullies."

"*Pushy?* I do hope you aren't gossiping about me Sissy!" Nikki glided over, looking like a runway model as always. Her dress was sleek, black and elegant, and her hair pulled up in a classic bun. She smiled slyly at Korban but he didn't acknowledge her glance, never mind the once-over she gives him, critically scanning him with her eyes. "Who's your *friend?* He's cute."

Sophie recalled her earlier conversation with her sister and suddenly wished Nikki was somewhere else. "Nikki, this is Korban Diego. Korban, this is my sister Nikki Winters."

"It's a pleasure to meet you. Sophie's told me *all* about *you*," Nikki's voice held a taunting lilt, but Korban knew it wasn't aimed at him.

There was something about Nikki that wasn't right to him. She smelled of perfume, and beauty, but underneath it all was the something callous, frozen. He had smelled this before on other people he had met, but it never had been this strong. It made her attractiveness shallow, almost ugly. Her smile that dazzled others reminded him instead of a dog baring its teeth. "Nice to meet you," he managed amicably. Regardless of her attitude, she was Sophie's sister and his mother had raised him with a gentleman's manners.

Nikki studied him, her eyes lingering as they trailed up and down his body, "So you're really a werewolf."

"*Nikki!*" Sophie hissed sharply at her sister, "don't be rude to my friend!"

His heart skipped a beat. Damn puppy love.

"What? I've never seen a lycanthrope so close before," she gazed into his eyes, observing him curiously.

Korban felt the hairs on the back of his neck raise. He didn't like the way she was looking at him, and he certainly did not like the way she spoke to him.

"Nikki! Stop!" Sophie's eyes narrowed, grabbing her sister by the arm. She looked at him, an apology written on her face. "I'm sorry, Korban. Excuse me for a moment."

He nodded. "Sure."

Sophie dragged her sister away, Nikki giving a wave as they parted ways. "Bye Korban. Nice meeting you."

"Bye," he said, relieved that Nikki was leaving but bummed as Sophie pardoned herself. Watching the two sisters weave through the crowd and to the ladies' room he let out a sigh. If he had met Nikki any other way he would have never guessed that the two were sisters. Not because their looks varied, but their scents… Sophie's smell was soft, warm, and alluring to him. Nikki's was plain and cold.

~*~

"I cannot believe you!" Sophie whirled around to glare at her sister as they duck into the ladies' room, flustered and angry. "How could you say something like that to him?"

"I was just trying to help, sissy. Don't be mad," Nikki shrugged. "Your husband's a slime ball for cheating on you. Korban seems nice. He's cute, like you said, and a hot body. And I'd bet he's an *animal* in bed!"

"Stop it! Please," Sophie put her fingers to her temples. "Tonight isn't about Lucas and I. It's about raising money for those kids, Nikki. I would appreciate it if you wouldn't embarrass me in front of my friends. He probably gets it enough from other people, and we're supposed to be civilized." She remembered how he'd told her it was difficult to even find a job.

"Look, I know you'd rather not think about it, but it pisses me off to think that he's creeping around while you play Martha Stewart around the house. I think you should have a bit of a thrill on the side, too."

"No, Nikki," Sophie shook her head, "I told you. I can't do that. I'm not like that."

"I'm sure your werewolf friend wouldn't mind," Nikki was pushing it. "After all, he was practically drooling on you when I came over."

"He was *not* drooling over me!" Sophie growled in exasperation, giving up. "Never mind. This- this is so childish. I'm going back out there. Try not to embarrass me again like that for the rest of the night, please?"

Nikki frowned. "I'm just trying to look after my sister, that's all."

"I can look after myself just fine, thank you." She made a frustrated noise, and rubbing her temples she headed toward the bathroom door.

~*~

Korban thought for sure that Sophie wasn't coming back. He was certain that she'd be too embarrassed, or something like that, to come near him for the rest of the night. He hadn't liked the way Nikki spoke to him and what was worse is maybe she scared Sophie off. Sophie had stuck up for him despite her sister's rude behavior, but he knew when his luck was running out.

Sighing, he wondered of RJ would mind leaving early. It was crowded enough but a few people seemed to glance his way and whisper to each other, and he began to feel that eerie paranoia that he was the center of attention because of his unusual eyes once again.

Thankfully, RJ was approaching, probably having witnessed what happened and Sophie's sudden departure with her sister. He was instantly glad he'd brought RJ instead of Alex with him- instead of teasing him on how it went, he gave Korban a comforting pat on the shoulder. "Hey, you okay?"

Korban nodded, managing a smile. "Yeah, I'll be fine. I mean, I wasn't even sure that I'd get a moment to speak with her again at all."

"You give yourself less credit than you should, Korban. You tend to leave an impression, you always have." RJ pat his shoulder. "We're here, why don't we go take advantage of the open bar? I think a few drinks may do us both a little good."

Korban raised an eyebrow as his smile turned genuine. "I thought open bars were more of Alex's thing."

"Hey, how often do you get a chance to smooze with Syracuse's higher society? Besides, I can't wait to rub Alex's face some more in what he's missing out of. That will teach him to taunt me when I'm grading midterms." He paused, something catching his attention and a lop-sided smirk forming on his lips. "Then again, I think I'll go enjoy the bar by myself. I don't want to become a third wheel. Have fun but not too much fun," RJ left, blending back into the crowd before Korban could say anything.

"Sorry I had to leave so abruptly again."

Sophie's voice made him turn in surprise. He grins more out of relief that she had returned than anything else. "It's okay."

"No, it isn't. I apologize for my sister's behavior, Nikki's always been an instigator." She sucked in a deep breath, gave him a sad smile. "I don't know how I am going to properly thank you when I have to keep apologizing."

"Well... you know how they do it in all the classic movies..." Korban suggested, eyes lighting up again with their usual mischief.

She gave him an incredulous look, eyebrows raised. He realized how he'd put it and laughed, embarrassed. His cheeks turned pink. "I meant- *oh!*" he stopped himself, trying not to laugh. "I meant a dance?"

"Oh!" Sophie turned an even darker shade of pink and began to laugh. "Oh well, in that case..."

He held out his hand with a charming grin. "May I have this dance?"

She took his hand and suddenly found herself in his arms. He felt so warm and he was so close... but instead of feeling like she was suffocating his nearness was comforting, like a favorite blanket. She felt safe and the feeling is unusual for her. She never trusted anyone so quickly before.

"I've always wanted to say that," he smiled to her and she laughed.

They began to dance to the slow jazz music the band was playing as the world around them faded away.

~*~

Not too far away RJ gave Korban a smile, and resisted the urge to flash him a thumbs-up. Okay, maybe he *had* spent too much time around Alex.

RJ scanned the crowd and saw that Lucas was beginning to emerge from the reporters, glancing around the room between interviews and obviously seeking out his wife. Afraid of what might happen, RJ quickly thought of a plan. "You so owe me, Korban," he muttered under his breath and then made a bee-line towards Lucas Bane, who had finally cleared away the reporters, who were now interested in flagging down the newest celebrity couple who just arrived.

RJ greeted Lucas even though he seemed preoccupied, scanning the crowd for Sophie. "Mr. Bane, I assume?"

Lucas smiled politely, smoothing over any impatience he may have had just moments ago in the pursuit of his wife. "That is correct," he paused, sticking out his hand, Lucas added, "Call me Lucas. And you sir are...?"

"Ramiel J. Ramirez," RJ firmly shook his hand. "I am a teacher at the Syracuse Alternative Middle School."

Something sparked in Lucas's eyes. Opportunity. "Really? I've heard that school is one of the worst in the city."

RJ smiled. He had his attention for now.

~*~

Alex would have been proud. Korban kept his hands right on her waist and was a total gentleman. He was no longer nervous, swaying slowly with Sophie in his arms. He was lost somewhere in the moment, not sure if this was real or just another dream.

Everyone else seemed to fade around them, he thought. Not just special effects in a movie. Something could feel so right that in the moment the rest of the world melted away.

She was married, which was horribly ironic. Because even though a part of him wished she was not, they never would have met had she not been married to Lucas. It was the cruelest thing he had been ever faced with, save for the night he had been turned.

He pushed that thought quickly aside. He didn't want to miss a single second of this lingering on the past. He wanted to remember this moment for the rest of his life.

The song ended and he reluctantly took a step away from her. Korban forced a smile, "I'd better give you back to your husband now."

She returned the smile as she pulled away. "Yeah." Silence fell between the two and nothing more could appropriately fill the blanks between them. She seemed a million miles away all over again. "Well... thank you. Enjoy the rest of the ball. Good night, Korban."

"Good night." Funny, it suddenly didn't feel that way to him anymore.

Korban scanned the room for RJ and found him with none other than Lucas Bane. *Better go rescue him.*

By the time he made his way through the crowd, RJ was parting ways and Lucas left to rejoin with his wife. RJ smiled at Korban. "I'd say you owe me, but Mr. Bane just gave me a check for our 3D printer."

"You have a 3D printer?"

"We do now," RJ grinned. "Well, I don't know about you, but this party is getting old fast- maybe we'd better get going before Alex decides to crash in."

The minute the words left his mouth the vast window across the room suddenly exploded, glass shattering as a snarling beast hit the ground. People screamed and began to scatter, covering their heads as they ran for cover. RJ swore. "Never should have opened my mouth."

Korban's jaw dropped open in horror as he identifies the intruder, confusion setting in. It wasn't even a full moon but he'd know that creature anywhere. Even if the last time he'd come face to face with one was on that fateful night five years ago, images flash through his mind, brief and terrible memories resurfacing. A massive canine-like creature stands before him on the dark street, like a nightmare come to life with its glowing yellow eyes and jet black fur. Pain lances through his collar as it moved too fast to see, a blur of shadowy fur knocking him violently to the pavement, razor-sharp teeth sinking in and damning him to this life as a- "Werewolf..." he stared in disbelief.

The beast was covered in oozing cuts, but they were already healing over as it shook its muddy brown fur, shards of glass clattering across the floor. The sound brings him back, a piece that is out of place since there was nothing like it that fit inside that dark memory. Korban watches as it sniffs the air, oddly calm despite the chaos that was erupting around it, almost appearing as if it was seeking something... or hunting someone. Its blood-red eyes glistened, focusing on a pretty blonde in a white evening gown-

Sophie Bane.

6: RESCUE

Before anyone could react the wolf lunged at the crowd. Short-lived screams echoed as it made its way through the mass of panicking party-goers, tearing apart anything in its way.

Letting out a roaring howl, the massive, bloody wolf leapt at its target, fangs sinking into Sophie's side. She screams, but it only blended with the chaotic chorus around them.

The monster easily lifted her in its mouth, as she kicked and wailed in pain. Then, just as quickly as it had come, the beast leapt off the stage and ran back towards the broken window with Sophie screaming in its jaws.

The Bane bodyguards fired their guns off at the beast but Lucas screamed for them to stop. *"You'll hit Sophie you idiots!!!"*

Korban pushed his way through the hysterical mass of people, fighting the current that was making its way toward the exit. Heart pounding and adrenaline rushing through his veins, Korban managed to leap through the shattered window, knocking loose a few remnants and landing on his feet. He heard Sophie's screams and could smell her blood. ***"Someone help!"*** She managed to scream between incoherent wails and sobs.

Korban took off like a bullet, heading through the maze of alleys, guided by his sense of smell and the echo of Sophie's screams. He turned a corner and saw the beast's shadow dart around the wall, a menacing blur lit only by the dim street lamp. With a snarl, he leapt at the wolf, clawing with his nails into the creature's eyes. The beast howled in pain, releasing Sophie. She fell to the ground sobbing as her blood began to pool on the pavement. The enraged creature roared and snapped its jaws viciously as its prey is stolen.

Korban bared his teeth at the creature. *"You can't have her!"* He bellowed, then with an amazing strength he never used before he threw the beast into the wall. Bricks cracked and crumbled at the force of the blow and the creature yelped like a wounded puppy.

It landed on its side and scrambled to its feet, its fierce red eyes squinting and shining in fear as it looked back at Korban. Its ears fall flat against its massive head and its tail curled up under its large body, assuming a submissive position in attempt to make itself as small as possible. Korban utters a low, inhuman growl and the beast flinched and yelped again, then turned and tore down the alley as fast as it could.

Korban rushed to where Sophie lay pale and trembling. He shreds a piece of her ruined dress to assess the bite, but the blood was pouring out too rapidly. He had to stop her side from bleeding. He used the fabric he tore from her dress and pressed it to her wounded side, praying that he hadn't been too late.

In the distance, sirens began to wail. He prayed for them to hurry. Sophie was making soft noises of pain and turned pale under the glow of the streetlight. Or was it the growing moon, nearly swollen to its full size? Three days away now.

The bleeding wouldn't stop. Korban tore off his suit jacket, already splattered in blood, and pressed it to her wound. He tossed the dress fabric that was soaked bright red with blood into the shadows of the alley. "Come on, Sophie. Hang on. Help is on the way."

The stench of fresh blood made something within him sickeningly hunger as well as invoke his fear, desperately urging him to flee. But suddenly he heard voices up the alleyway. Glancing up, he was about to yell for help when he caught wind of their conversation.

"Where's the target?" A female's voice asked sharply, the tinny sound of technology hinting to Korban that her voice was coming over a cell phone.

"She's nearby. She's weak and she's lost a lot of blood. I doubt she'll survive the night." A man's voice this time, closer and clearer.

"There's doubt and then there's certainty. You better not screw this up."

Heart thudding in his chest, Korban tried to be still and listened very carefully to their conversation as he continued to apply pressure to Sophie's bleeding wound.

Fear entered the male's voice. "The Boss warned us not to leave too many bodies behind."

Boss? Someone was hired to make sure Sophie was dead?!

"Yeah, so what does that have to do with anything?"

The male took in a deep breath, then exhaled. "She's not alone. Whoever she is with scared off the Wolven."

The female swore. "Even if someone's with her, even if she escapes, she's probably as good as dead anyway. Follow them to the hospital and finish her off with a silver bullet when no one's watching if she makes it. Don't mess this up or it's both our hides."

"And what should I do about the beast? Do you want me to track it down and finish it?"

"No. Let the police dispose of it, if they can find it. It'll make better headlines if they actually stop it."

Cold fear crawled up Korban's spine. What had he just overheard? Sophie moaned and his attention returned to her. It was Sophie who was in danger right now.

"Don't worry, Sophie. I'm getting you out of here," Korban vowed in a whisper as he wrapped his suit jacket around her and carefully scooped her up into his arms. A breeze picked up and he could smell a familiar scent coming from up the alley, and instantly knew whose footsteps were suddenly racing towards them. RJ came tearing down the alley, faster than Korban had ever seen him go.

"There you are, Korban." RJ panted. "I was looking everywhere for you, oh God, Sophie- we need to get her to the hospital."

Korban vehemently shook his head, hissing in a low, hurried whisper, "No, we can't do that RJ."

"What?! What do you mean we can't-"

"There's no time to explain. The police and ambulance will be here any second. We have to be gone by then."

"But Sophie-"

"She'll be fine if she stays with us. Someone's after her and they'll kill her if she goes to the hospital. We have to go now, before it's too late."

The sirens were drawing nearer and he could hear voices and hurried footsteps; the clicking and snapping of guns being loaded with silver bullets. Korban pleads to RJ, shifting Sophie's unconscious form in his arms. "Please, you have to trust me. I'll explain back home."

RJ reluctantly caved. "Okay, go. I'll meet you there." He rushed back up the alley to go get their car.

Korban tore off like a flash, leaping up the fire escapes and along the top of the buildings, holding Sophie close to his chest. Every few minutes he would alter his path, check to see if he was being followed. He went with the wind to catch any scent of a stalker but only the scent of the city seemed to trail them. He'd lost them, whoever they were. Racing to the garage, leaping from rooftop to rooftop, he felt thankful for being a werewolf for the first time since he was first attacked.

~*~

Alex sighed heavily. Paperwork was definitely not his thing, but he'd suffer through it as long as possible. RJ usually helped him out but instead tonight his two roommates were living lifestyles of the rich and famous. However RJ deserved it after a rough week of teaching, and Alex knew better than anyone how stressed RJ could get. The break in routine was well earned. He hoped they were having a good time.

The piles of papers were practically glaring at him it seemed, if such a thing was possible. After this was done, he thought to himself, he'd have a beer then go to bed. Physical labor won against a mountain of paperwork any day.

Suddenly the door burst open. Alex jumped to his feet in surprise as Korban rushes into the apartment, carrying an unconscious Sophie Bane in his arms. "What the hell?" Alex blinked at the two of them in total shock and awe. "Having a good time without me, huh?"

RJ was in teacher-mode as he rushed in from behind, face flushed from running, the car's engine still rumbling in the garage.

"Clear off the table, get some towels and the first aid kit."

It was then Alex noticed the blood over Sophie's dress and Korban's shirt. He turned the color of chalk and froze. "Oh my God." Panicking, he knocked everything clear from the kitchen table and grabs towels and the first aid kit from the linen closet. "What happened? Should I call 911?"

"No," Korban stated firmly. "Under normal circumstances I would say that we should call for an ambulance but we can't. The moment she steps foot in a hospital she's dead." RJ threw the first thing he could grab over the table- a worn blanket normally used to cover their worn couch.

"She's really not looking good," Korban laid her gently onto the table and tore his shirt off, pressing it to her wound. His skin was sticky and wet in some areas from her blood soaking through. "She could bleed to death at this rate!"

"I don't think she'll bleed to death Korban," RJ said in a hushed tone. Korban turned to give him a look, and his friend's skin was ashen. "Look at her."

It was odd, but he smelled the change before he saw it. Suddenly Sophie's alluring scent was almost overpowering, intoxicating. He couldn't help but breathe in deeply, the vanilla and minty smell suddenly flowery and wilder than before. Looking down he watched in horrified wonder as her wounds began to heal, slowly closing before their eyes. The bleeding had stopped and he could hear the rhythm of her heart strengthen with every beat.

A lump formed in his throat and his mouth went dry, cold dread filling him. Sophie would live, just as he had after his attack five years ago. And the next full moon night, only days from now, she would change just like he did. She was like him now. He feels a small thrill run deep inside of him, something that exhilarated and disgusted him at the same time.

He felt cold, turning to RJ and Alex, both of his human friends looking pale and worried. He wondered if he looked like a monster to them at that moment, he wasn't sure what expression had frozen upon his face. Perhaps he was a bit of a monster for that glorious thought. Or maybe he was human for it. "We should get her cleaned up," Korban said softly. "Can you get some washcloths? When she wakes it will be better if she doesn't have to see her own blood everywhere." Or smell it, he thought grimly.

As if in a trance Alex nodded. His friend had no witty comeback to this and Korban was thankful for it. RJ helped him sponge the blood off Sophie, then helped get one of his huge old t-shirts over her and remove what remained of her once lovely ball gown. Korban helped carry her to his bedroom and tucked her under the covers, watching her rest for a moment before returning out to the kitchen, where RJ and Alex were cleaning off the table where Sophie had bled only minutes before. Or had it been hours? He'd completely lost all track of time since the moment the monstrous wolf had crashed the party.

They sat together at the small card table for a long moment, still shell-shocked from the entire night's events. No one said anything. Korban heard his two friends' breath hitch as a siren went past. Finally, Alex broke the silence. "I guess I'll put on some coffee. This is going to be a long night."

Korban chuckled mirthlessly, rubbing his temples. RJ nodded. "Coffee is nice, but an explanation would be better. What happened in that alley Korban? Why are we now holding Sophie hostage instead of taking her to the emergency room?"

"Someone was in that alley on a cell phone. A man talking with a woman. They were talking about her attack and said how someone had set it up. Their 'Boss'. They were supposed to let the wolf finish her off, but I was there." Korban couldn't shake the eerie feeling of being hunted. The Wolf inside of him was on alert. The adrenaline was still rushing through his veins and he wanted to calm down, to be able to think clearly and to be able to protect Sophie from whoever was hunting her down. "All I know is they would have finished the job if they didn't already think she was dying. I know if I wasn't there to stop the beast, it would have torn her apart. Or help would have come and that guy would have put a silver bullet in her if she made it to the hospital. I wasn't going to let them near her." It struck him then, and he growled. "They would stop at nothing to kill her."

RJ frowned. "Why would anyone be after Sophie Bane?"

"I don't know! All I know is what I heard. They could have wanted money or fame," the thought made Korban sick to his stomach. "How could anyone agree to such a thing?"

"I... I wish I had the answer, but the fact is I have no idea," RJ said softly, "but, what I do know is everyone and their mother is going to be looking for her tomorrow morning, including the entire police force."

"If they aren't already now," Alex amended, frowning worriedly.

Korban sighed. "I know, I know. But she was set up to die in that alley. If she goes home they'll know she's alive and try to attack her again and we won't be there to stop it. She could die."

"Korban, this is a very serious situation. Lucas Bane- and her family- they'll be looking for her. They're probably worried sick. They have the right to know that she is going to be okay. Well, that she survived the attack anyway," RJ insisted with a very stern, serious look. "You can't hide away someone's wife, mother, daughter from the world." Then it dawns on him and RJ pauses, the look on his face one of clarity as he realizes the fact of the matter. "If she even survives her first change, Korban. She may only have a few days left to live. She should have the chance to say goodbye to her family if the lycanthropy kills her. Besides, don't you think the press will blame you for her turning into a werewolf if we don't do something?"

"Me?! That's ridiculous! Everyone saw that beast grabbing her!" The very idea was preposterous.

"Still, if the media doesn't link it to you, Lucas Bane might," Alex looked worried. "I don't mean to be pessimistic, just realistic. Suppose we do return her safely and everyone gets the wrong idea..."

As his friend's voice trails off, Korban lets the statement hang in the air for a moment before he shakes his head. "Sophie is in danger, but this should be up to her. It's her choice on what she wants to do next. The only thing I can do- that *we* can do- is to help her get through this."

"Only time will tell, but I hope we can help her," RJ sighs, his brow creased in thought. "For now, I think it's best we all sleep on it. Maybe Sophie can enlighten us when she wakes in the morning to any enemies she or her husband may have. Being wealthy and powerful makes you a target for a lot of people and maybe there is more to this than it seems. But at this hour even with coffee we won't be able to solve this. So let's at least try to get a few z's and reassemble after breakfast."

Everyone nodded in unison. It was hard to argue with RJ's logic, especially with a couple hours left until morning.

Glancing around the now clean table that only a few moments ago Sophie had bled upon, they dismissed the meeting without another word.

7: REPERCUSSIONS

Korban was laying on the couch and just started to drift off when the phone blared to life. The sound, ringing intensified as it was, made him jump and grit his teeth as he picks it up and mumbles, "Hello?"

An even wearier voice came from the other line. "Korban, it's Sergeant McKinnon."

Shit. Not using his first name on a call meant Tim was being official and calling him on business. Korban's heart speeds up. "I'm going to stop by first thing in the morning. I have some questions about tonight but it doesn't look like I'll be leaving this scene any time soon."

Korban's mouth goes dry and he sits up, rubbing his temples. "You know I wouldn't. I couldn't. It's not even a full moon."

Tim's guffaw comes from the other end, but it is short lived. "Korban, we'd be having a different conversation and not over the phone if I thought you were behind this mess. I just need to get a statement from you and RJ tomorrow. Regarding your presence at this ball and a couple other things."

"All right man. You know where to find us," Korban is sure his ability to sleep was now null and void.

"Make sure you stay put tonight," Tim cautions, then says a bit softer, "Oh and Korban? You may want to lay low the next few days. The shit storm is bound to hit from all this. I'll explain more when I'm by tomorrow."

~*~

Since sleep was off the table for that night Korban spent a majority of the time either pacing, cleaning, or obsessing over what Tim was going to grill him on. What would he tell him if he asked about last night's events? Sophie was still sound asleep, the infection coursing through her veins. Every moment she was changing, her human cells morphing into stronger ones, cells meant to endure the monthly cycle of transformation.

He sat on the couch, his head in his hands. Should he get a story ready? No, Tim was a friend, and maybe... Would he understand the truth? RJ was there and almost didn't believe him.

He paces in the living room, trying in vain to sort his thoughts. The walls seem to be closing in on him so he heads up the short flight of stairs to the rooftop. The chill in the night air feels like cool silk against his skin. The tightness in his chest eases a bit with each breath. Familiar scents of home calm him as much as the restless beast within. He catches the scent of Sophie's blood and his stomach forms a knot.

He feels at a loss, sitting on the roof, the woman of his dreams laying bitten in his bed. He would have never, ever wished this upon anyone. Least of all Sophie.

While he contemplates how to even talk to her about what came next, a squad car pulls up and Tim steps out, gazing up to him and giving a wave. Korban waves back and Tim's weary eyes peer from his sunglasses. Clearly they'd both had no sleep between the two of them. "Be right down," Korban stands and Tim nods, yelling back, "I hope ya have coffee on!"

Once they'd settled around the kitchen table, coupled with fresh mugs of coffee, Tim takes a long swig, then studies Korban. "Long night too, huh?"

"Yeah," Korban takes a sip of his own but barely tastes it. Tim was fishing for information and he wouldn't rise to the bait if he could help it. "Hard to get a good night's rest when you've witnessed something so surreal, even for a werewolf."

Tim smirks at that, sipping his coffee again. "I'm glad we knew each other before all this mess, otherwise I'm not sure I'd believe someone was that incredibly…"

"Creative?" Korban supplies.

"I was gonna go with unlucky," Tim chuckles, then he sighs and leans closer, "We've already established that you were at the party last night, and I know RJ was there too in order to vouch for you."

Shit. Why did he feel suddenly guilty when it wasn't even his fault. He'd been a heroic passerby when Sophie was attacked. Perhaps because he knew that he was about to lie to a man who always had his back.

Even so, what choice did he have at the moment? Even telling the truth seemed reaching. Showing an unconscious, newly infected Sophie who was laying in his bed- well that would be hard to pass off as *not* his fault. And then Sophie would be in danger, caged and in quarantine with those prying cold eyes and calculated looks…

"I also know you, Korban. I know you have never transformed outside the cycle of the full moon. Which makes me wonder if you were set up."

This takes him by surprise, his mind going blank and he blinks, staring at Tim in mild disbelief as he digests those words. "What?" was the first thing to come to his lips.

Tim shifts his weight from one foot to another and nods, his expression remaining serious. "I'll be honest. You being invited there, then a werewolf attacking... I don't believe in coincidences, Korban. I'm looking into who invited you. Someone wanted you there, and in a bad way."

With everything he overheard, and now this, it did make him wonder. "Lucas Bane, he invited me. He offered me a position with his company, just a start up thing, probably as a janitor or something. He wanted me at the party to... well, he claimed to lessen the shock of me being a werewolf and all to the other employees," Korban rubs his temples, sinking in his seat a little. "What... what should I do?"

"Nothing. Lay low, and for now... I'll get your formal statement. This is gonna hit the fan fast and the sooner was cross our T's and dot our I's the better. For your sake as well as RJ's, and mine." Tim flips open a pad of paper. "So, walk me through what happened last night."

~*~

Sophie was on stage alone, the spotlight hot and bright over her. Sweat beaded on her forehead as she tried to focus on anyone familiar in the dark theater beyond the stage. There was the sound of shuffling programs and shifting seats out in the shadowy auditorium. Somewhere in the packed audience a man cleared his throat and anxious murmurs began to fill the air, growing louder and louder.

She tapped the mic and its squeaky feedback made her cringe. She tried to speak but her mouth was dry and unable to form words.

The murmuring grew louder as the audience quickly grew impatient. She desperately looked off stage for an exit but the curtains were gone, solid chains hanging in their place. The crowd began to jeer and she pleaded into the mic, "I... I'm sorry, I can't do this..."

Suddenly a large red object flew at her from the agitated audience. It splattered red all over her white dress, then thudded wetly on the stage. More and more tomatoes flew from the upset crowd and exploded on the stage around her, the jeering becoming a tidal wave of disapproval that filled the concert hall.

She covered her face with her arms and the jeers suddenly became growls. Peering at the audience she saw hundreds of glowing red eyes. A tomato splattered near her and she watched as it came to rest by her shoe. Her eyes widened.

They hadn't been throwing tomatoes at all, she realized in horror as she stared down at the still beating, bloody heart laying at her feet.

~*~

She woke, jolting upright and immediately regretting the move as pain lanced up her side. Her heart was racing and she glanced over herself, still feeling the warm blood that had covered her in the dream.

She shuddered at the thought of hearts being thrown at her, even more sickened by the fleeting thought of how she'd wanted to bite into one of them.

The door opened and his scent struck her even before she glanced up at Korban. This startled her and for a moment she stiffened and leapt back, away from him. Just as abruptly came the memories of last night, images flashing before her eyes. The monstrous wolf shattering through the window, grabbing her in its jaws and tearing into her still pain-wrought side; Korban slamming the beast into the wall, protecting her; then how he held her while she bled in the alley, after scaring the beast away.

He looked relieved to see her and he carefully approached. "Sophie... you okay?"

"I've been better," she croaked and almost laughed, but her sarcasm was stifled by his alluring scent. Forrest, sanctuary. Feelings evoked by his smell, which was distinct and indescribable. She felt safer than she could remember and the terrible nightmare was suddenly far away. Just a bad dream.

Her throbbing side was all too real, though, and she pulled up her shirt, glancing at the bandages. "I thought I'd wake up in a hospital, if I woke up at all," she shivered at her own words. Korban sat in the chair beside her bed, offering a glass of water that almost magically appeared, as she did not notice it in his hand before. She took it and gulped it down, thankful to get rid of the itchy, cotton-dry feeling from her throat. The wooden chair he sat upon seemed out of place in the room but smelled of him, as if he had recently spent a lot of time in it. "How long have I been unconscious?"

"Two days," he admitted, gazing worriedly over her. "I would have taken you to the hospital but I overheard someone in the alley. They... they knew you were supposed to be attacked. That you were to be killed."

His words sent a chill through her, and she could tell by the intense look in his eyes that he was not lying. A lump formed in her throat when the knowledge struck her. Of course she had survived her attack, but now... everything was different. But saying it out loud would make it tangible, real. She did not want to face that nightmare, not yet. "Two days," she repeated, then gasped. "Daniel," Sophie got up, hissing as the muscles jerked and agitated her healing side, but she was determined to get moving. "I have to get home. I can't just abandon my son, not like this."

"Wait, please," Korban insisted, sympathy reflected in his eyes. "You have to understand something. It's not that easy to just go home."

Sophie tensed, her eyes narrowing. "Are you trying to keep me captive here, Korban?"

He paled, eyes going round. "No, no. Never. I'm just trying to protect you, Sophie. I know you can smell it, everything around here, even yourself, it's different. You've been bitten by a werewolf."

Of course she'd known that, but the moment he said it she froze. "I know that. But I'm fine, and you were fine that night at the bar, and here now, and even before at the party right? And it'll be okay, I can deal with the whole… full moon thing when it comes up."

"In one more day," Korban pointed out, frowning. "Which means it's going to be even more difficult for you. It's going to happen fast."

"What's going to happen fast?" Sophie folded her arms over her chest, demanding answers and wondering if he was just trying to keep her there longer.

"The days leading up to the full moon, when you're infected, your body adjusts slowly. But when you've been bitten only a few days before… I don't know what is going to happen, but your eyes have already started to change." Korban paused. "It's not just your eyes and sense of smell that have been altered. You'll feel things you hadn't experienced before, things that will make you sick to your stomach. Things that will make you wonder if you've lost your mind, or become a monster."

Sophie stared at him. "I feel fine now."

"Which I don't understand, but you should be careful, or at least know what could happen." Korban seemed to be worried about something.

She felt oddly numb and was sure that she was in shock, and maybe the world would come crashing down later. Werewolf or not, she had survived that brutal attack and her family must be worried sick about her if she'd been hidden away for the past two days. "Tell me what I need to know then, Korban," she met his gaze, able to see the variations of gold flecks that made up the amber in his eyes. It was as if her vision had been blurred for her entire life until now, and she could finally see everything in high definition.

"I never knew a werewolf before I was bitten five years ago. I'm the only werewolf I really know personally even now. So I'm not sure if it will be different for you, but I wanted you to at least have fair warning." Korban sucked in a deep breath and she could hear the sound inflate his lungs, "I'm in control of myself now. But it took a couple years to get where I am now."

Sophie watched him, listening. She leaned against the wall, favoring her good side to keep her sore side alleviated. She was grateful that the pain was already subsiding. She wasn't sure where he was going with this whole issue of control. She felt fine, save for her aching bite wound. "It may have taken you a couple years Korban, but I'm telling you that right now I feel just fine. I'm worried about my family and it isn't right if they think I'm hurt somewhere, lost or worse. I can't do that to Daniel, or Lucas. Even if he's done some terrible things. I can't put him through that kind of deception."

Korban's gaze remained worried, his mouth a thin line. "Somebody set you up, Sophie. They purposely sent that monster after you, to kill you, and they would have if I wasn't there. I'm afraid of what they'll do if they find out you survived the attack. Someone is after you- a man and a woman who are working for somebody- and I don't know who they are, but they have to be pretty sick and desperate to have thought up something like this for your execution."

Sophie's hands trembled, curling into fists. "I'm not scared. I think I could take them on, easy." The sudden boost of confidence was empowering and also frightening. She was never a violent person before. Had surviving this attack really changed her that much? She didn't care. Right now her priority was as it always was, to her family, especially her son. She moved to the door, her side only flaring up with an echo of pain compared to what it was when she first woke. "I thank you for taking care of me, Korban. It means a lot, but I have to go. Good bye."

He didn't get up when she reached for the door, only giving her a pained, worried look. He was genuinely afraid for her, wanting her to be safe. Normally her conscience would kick in but she didn't feel like being a cowardly kicked puppy anymore. She had a second chance at life and she wasn't about to waste it like she had the first time.

The moment she stepped outside of the room, there was an explosion of sounds and smells, as if someone suddenly cranked the volume to full blast. The tinny sound of metal grating against metal, of a familiar song blaring all too loudly on the radio; the smell of sweat, testosterone, oil, gasoline and the pungent aroma of garbage- a rotting banana peel, moldy bread, tuna fish and soured mayonnaise- that was oddly interesting instead of stomach churning. The light pouring in through the windows illuminated a world that was too focused, almost giving her a headache. She could see every fiber on the couch, and the worn carpet of the floor. The air was so full of dancing specs of dust she wanted to hold her breath to keep them at bay from her lungs. The apartment reeked of Korban but two others as well, one who smelled of oil and gasoline and another who smelled of paper, chalk, and ink. It was an explosion, an overload of information to all of her senses and she froze, immobile, overwhelmed by it all.

The sound of a lock clicking was as loud as a shotgun blast and her gaze went to it instantly. A man who she vaguely remembered from the bar the other night walked in, a backwards cap poised on his head, wiping his hands on an oil-stained rag. Their eyes met and he grinned mischievously, almost as if he was baring his teeth to her as he approached. His mouth moved, he was saying something, but his wet, thumping heartbeat reminded her of her dream. The rush of his blood in his veins and the delectable scent that rolled from him made her mouth water. She wasn't staring at a man anymore. In her mind he was prey, the thick artery in his throat pulsing just beneath his skin.

"Sophie, no!" Korban cried out and her human side wondered for a moment why.

It happened so very fast. One moment she was across the room, watching this familiar stranger's pulse in his neck. The next she had him pinned to the wall, her lips curled back in a snarl, her nostrils flaring, drinking in the fear that suddenly radiated from him, making him all the more appealing to eat. Her teeth actually grazed the skin when suddenly strong arms were around her, the scent of forest and fur and male pulling her away from her prey. For a moment she was angry, struggling against him, angry that he was trying to steal her prey. Then after a few deep mouthfuls of the air that was strong with wolf scent, she calmed, trembling with a fear of her own as she saw the expression on the man's face. There were red marks where her teeth had grazed his throat but thankfully she hadn't broken the skin.

"Oh my God," Sophie gasped, sagging against Korban and catching a whiff of her almost-victim's fear. The distinct tang of urine was in the air, and she knew without seeing that she literally had scared the piss out of Alex.

She struggled again, only this time she didn't want to go after him. She wanted to flee the room. Korban pulled her back into the bedroom, closing the door behind them and with the click of the hinges the world outside was shut out.

Sophie couldn't stop shaking, wrapping her arms around

herself. Tears began to roll down her cheeks, and she could smell the salt in them. "What's wrong with me?"

Korban gazed to her sympathetically. "I'm sorry you had to find out the hard way, but we're lucky nothing permanent happened."

"I almost bit your roommate!" Sophie yelped. "I wanted to eat him! I can't be around people, not like this!" Then she eyed him suspiciously. "Why don't I want to attack you?"

"Maybe because I'm the same as you," Korban shrugged. "I honestly don't know. You're the first werewolf I've come in contact with since I was bitten. I wasn't looking to run into any others, honestly. I was just trying to do what I could to get on with my life."

"I can't," Sophie sobbed. "I can't go back. Not like this, Korban. I could seriously hurt someone, or worse." Now that she could think her stomach churned at the thought of almost sinking her teeth into human flesh. She sat down on the bed, still holding herself, rocking a little. "What am I supposed to do? I can't go back home like this." She couldn't bring herself to admit her true fear of that terrifying moment- that she could easily do the same thing to her own son.

Korban went over and sat in the chair across from her, his knee nearly touching hers. He reeked of sadness and sympathy. "Tomorrow night is the full moon. After that you might go back to normal again, and it will be much easier to control until the next full moon."

Sophie didn't miss a beat. "So you're saying that there is a chance that even after the full moon, I could be like this." The thought sent a fresh chill through her spine.

Korban nodded grimly, gazing apologetically to her. "I hope not, but it is a possibility. Like I said, I only know my own experience from being bitten and my own transformations."

She bowed her head and let the salty tears fall, her hands hanging between her knees as she slumped forward in grief. "Who would want to do this to me? It's worse than being killed."

His hand was suddenly upon hers and she glanced up through her tear-blurred eyes, seeing the sorrow in his amber eyes. "I don't know who did this, Sophie. But I promise you, after we deal with the full moon, I'm going to hunt them down myself. I won't rest until I find out who is behind this, I swear it."

~*~

It broke Korban's heart to watch Sophie cry herself to sleep. He stayed in the bedroom for a long time afterward, afraid to leave her alone. He knew this wasn't easy firsthand, and it was going to be hell for her for at least the next twenty four hours. There was a light knocking on the door when he was just about to doze off and he jerked up, awake. Sophie stirred a little in her sleep, but then went still again as exhaustion took hold of her once more. He got up and went over to the door before the culprit could knock again and disrupt Sophie's sleep. RJ was cautiously peering in, a worried look in his eyes. "Come out, we need to talk."

Korban nodded and reluctantly left the room, slowly closing the door behind him. "I know Alex must have told you what happened. She's sleeping now. The full moon is tomorrow night, if she can get through that, maybe she'll have a shot at a somewhat normal life too."

"We can only hope. In the meantime, Alex and I are going to keep our distance. Two werewolves under one roof is going to be difficult enough, we don't need either of us to get infected too. It's going to be difficult enough to explain this mess, and eventually Sophie is going to have to find a handler to claim her... once this mess is all sorted out." RJ leads him into the kitchen where there was a pile of sandwiches on a platter. "I made you and Sophie lunch. Piled them high with meat and cheese, hopefully once her hunger is sated she'll be a little more personable."

Korban smirked despite himself, but said seriously, "She can't help herself. Right now the wolf is gaining control over her, and quickly. What normally takes a week she is doing in hours. Cut her some slack."

"I will, only because she's your dream girl," Alex strode in from the garage, still looking a little pale, but otherwise recovered with that same mischievous smile as always spread across his face. "Though you better have a chat with her. I'm not into the rough stuff."

"You keep it up, I'll give you rough stuff," Korban growled playfully, then picked up the platter of sandwiches. He glanced over to Alex. "She feels bad enough about it as it is. Please don't tease her just yet about all of this. It's a lot for her to swallow. Her whole world's been shaken. Once we tackle the first hurdle, we're going for them next. I want to find out who set Sophie up, and make them pay."

RJ frowned worriedly. "Revenge is never the answer."

Korban glanced to him. "I don't plan on doing it myself. I'm not that crazy. I just want to find evidence of who set up Sophie and then let the cops lock them up." Of course he hoped he could control himself when he did get his hands on whoever was responsible. "Whoever is sick enough to think something like this up deserves to rot in a prison cell."

"One thing at a time then," RJ sighed, rubbing his temples in an attempt to fend off a headache. "The full moon first, then you may drag us into another one of your adventures."

Korban grinned at that, though his gaze went distant as he thought. "I hope Sophie makes it through the transformation," he confessed softly.

"I do too," Alex said grimly, his smile fading. "She will, Korban. She has you with her to help her through this, after all."

"Yeah," Korban wasn't as certain, but seeing Alex's hopeful look did lift his spirits. He managed a smile and nodded to them. "Thank you. Both of you, for everything."

"You're welcome. Hopefully Sophie will like the sandwiches too." Alex beamed, then winked. "I'm sure they taste a heck of a lot better than I would."

~*~

Sophie opened her eyes the moment he closed the door behind him and tentatively sniffing the air. Her eyes lit up when she saw the pile of food on the tray. "Are we expecting company?" She asked a bit nervously, worried about a repeat performance of earlier after seeing how many sandwiches were piled up on the platter.

"No, it's just me and you," he held out the tray in offering, smiling to her. "One of the few perks of being a werewolf is our speedy metabolism. It allows us to heal faster and eat just about as much of anything that we want without gaining a pound. Of course, it's quite a blow to the budget to feed a werewolf. Probably worse than feeding the three of us together as teenagers."

Sophie picked a thick sandwich off the top of the pile, stuffed with turkey and ham and took a bite. The meat was satisfying but smelled oddly old but new at the same time, and it made her wrinkle her nose a little. Korban gave her a knowing smile. "Lunch meat is carrion to our noses. It's still good, but not quite fresh enough for the wolf side, even if it is fresh for the human part."

She nodded, even after the first few bites still finding herself ravenous. She devoured the sandwich in just a few moments then went for another. Every bite made her feel better, less shaky and more focused. As if reading her thoughts he said, "Food helps a lot. Full bellies make happy werewolves."

Giving him a quick smile, Sophie went for a third sandwich, then a fourth. By the fifth she calmed down and he handed her a bottle of water. She blushed, feeling embarrassed to have eaten so much so quickly. "Thank you," she twisted the bottle cap, glancing to him. "You saved my life, and you've been so kind to me, even though we barely know each other."

"I couldn't just let that Wolven run off with you. Not when I knew I could do something. I was probably the only one there who could," Korban picked up a sandwich, taking a bite and swallowing it. "At least the only one with nothing to lose if a werewolf turned on them. You were screaming and crying and I couldn't just stand by and do nothing while…" he trailed off, shuddering, his eyes going intense as that night when he'd challenged Lucas' thug in the bar. "Anyway, you're safe now. That's all that matters."

Her cheeks burned. When he looked at her that way, her stomach filled with butterflies. She busied herself with her bottle cap again. "You're a very honorable man, Korban," she said softly, meeting those amber eyes shyly. "Your mother must be proud."

The look in his eyes sobered and he averted his gaze, his smile turning a little sad. "Yeah, I'm sure she would be."

"Oh no! I'm so sorry. I didn't realize that your mother passed away," Sophie apologized quickly, feeling terrible to bring up his painful loss.

"It's okay, really. It was a long time ago now," Korban paused. "She was a good woman and she died young. I was just thirteen at the time. Pops took me in and became my legal guardian because no one really wanted me in my own family."

"Pops?" She wondered if that was his grandfather.

"Alex's grandfather. Alex is one of my roommates, the one you, um… ran into earlier." She felt her cheeks warm again but he only laughed. "It's okay. He's fine, just shaken up but he'll recover. No harm done and we can prevent that from happening by staying away from them until after the full moon. By then hopefully you'll be okay enough to be properly introduced."

Sophie smiled. "I would like that."

This was nice, to sit here and have a normal conversation with her new friend. Even if her nose tingled from all the smells in the room, and her ears were overwhelmed by the breath escaping and filling their lungs. Her sense of smell even more acute than when she'd been pregnant with Daniel, all of her senses were more incredible than ever before. Which reminded her, "I'm sorry for taking your bedroom from you."

He cracked another smile. "I'm not too surprised you figured that out. This is the quietest room in the apartment. It used to be a bomb shelter of some sort which is why it's more comfortable in here- the sounds are muted by the thick walls," he pauses and apologizes, "Sorry if it makes you uncomfortable at all, staying here in my room."

"Not at all," Sophie feels her cheeks burn as it occurs to her how it wasn't the quiet that comforted her, as much as the fact that his scent was everywhere around her here. Something about his wild forest scent calmed her. "It's strangely comforting actually. But I do feel a little guilty taking over your room like this."

"It's okay, I'd rather you be comfortable as you can be right now," Korban finished the last sandwich, but she caught his grin. She remembered what Nikki said and her stomach did a flip. Maybe he did have a crush on her after all. She wasn't sure how to react to this discovery.

True, he was handsome, and now he was more than just the hero for the night. He'd saved her life and he was here with her now, the only person she could talk to without trying to devour. She was still married but Lucas was unfaithful. She had enough evidence to convince herself of that heartbreaking betrayal. It seemed wrong to think of any other men, especially after committing to her marriage vows. Even more so now that they shared a son together and were a family. She didn't believe in getting revenge. The whole an eye for an eye thing never appealed to her. Even with the hurt she felt from her cheating husband, she could never bring herself to use another human being like that. Especially Korban, who could have easily taken advantage of the circumstance but instead was genuinely concerned for her and helping her through this extremely difficult situation.

Korban, who was watching her with that primal look that made her tingle inside. "What's on your mind?" he asked with a slight tilt of his head.

She wondered for a moment what to tell him, but decided instead to simply say, "You."

His scent seemed to grow stronger at that, more alluring than before. It would be so easy to give in and just lean in and kiss him where he sat, only inches away from her. He wanted it even more than she did. "What about me?" Even his voice had deepened with his desire.

She couldn't lead him on like this, even if a big part of her now wanted nothing more than to pursue these feelings. "How you've been able to handle all this, by yourself, for five years now. You must have been attacked during the initial outbreak."

He hesitates, shuddering at the memory. "What came after was worse."

She doesn't speak, even when he pauses, his brow knitting in a way that made her realize that whatever had been "after" really was bad, and something he still struggled with even now. He takes a heavy breath and begins, "After you survive the initial attack, they run tests, and while they wait for the results… they put you in quarantine."

She gives a small nod, remembering it from the news during those early days. There was something chilling in the haunted look that took over his usually warm gold eyes. "Instead of a hospital back then, they brought me to this facility… they converted this psychiatric ward and…" He gazes to her and sighs. "I don't want you to have to go through it. To have your world turned upside down is bad enough. I… I know now I was one of the lucky ones. I got out of there because RJ is a good guy, my best friend and willing to sponsor me as a handler. Not everyone has someone who can do that. Not everyone escapes quarantine. Not everyone survives the first change, or even the first bite. I wasn't even thinking werewolf when the black wolf attacked me in the alley. I thought it was a huge rabid dog." His paused and glances down. "My best friend Ace was killed in the attack."

She just couldn't help but continue to hurt him, could she? This poor man had been dealt a rough hand at life. Losing his mother young, his best friend, and almost his own life. Now he was cursed with the same thing that would have her howling at the moon tomorrow night. "I'm so sorry again. I can't seem to think of anything we can talk about that won't bring up bad memories for you."

Korban only smiled. "It's okay, really. I don't mean to be a downer. You're right, it is a lot to handle. The way I see it though, I still have my two good friends, who are really more like brothers to me. And besides, if all the bad luck has passed, that means only good luck is left, right?"

He really was an amazing person, to have such a positive outlook after experiencing so much pain and sorrow. It was inspiring, and she couldn't help but return his smile. "I hope you're right."

"I hope so, too."

8: REVELATIONS

As the sun set that evening the growing moon came into view from the window and Sophie started to pace. This close to the full moon Korban knew what it was like with the wolf so near the surface. It felt like being trapped. His senses were so alive and yet confined to the brick and metal of a building, when all he really wanted to do was run and breathe in fresh grass, trees, and wildlife. Sophie had left the room only one other time cautiously to use the restroom and only after making sure that Alex was safely down in the garage.

An idea popped into his mind. He couldn't take her to the forest, but maybe some fresh air would help her relax a little. She was still resting in his room when he revealed his plan to RJ and Alex, who had mixed reactions to his idea. "Are you sure it's safe?" Alex asked, even more reluctant than RJ for a change.

Korban nodded. "If you are both in the garage when I take her up to the roof, then you'll be out of harm's way. We won't be up there very long, there could be search planes or helicopters out there. I think a little fresh air will do her good. She's not a prisoner, we're trying to keep her safe and comfortable here until... until she's ready to make a decision about what to do next."

Alex hesitated, exchanging a glance with RJ, who nodded.

"I'll help you clean up the garage for a little bit. That should give you about a half hour, Korban. Just to be safe," RJ paused, then added, "If you see a low flying plane, a spotlight, or helicopter, get inside quickly. It's bad enough that you'll probably be on *America's Most Wanted* sooner or later."

Though he was joking, Korban didn't miss the hint. "Sooner or later?" he repeated, raising an eyebrow in question.

RJ frowned. "You were the only known werewolf at the party and personally invited by Lucas Bane. Frankly, I'm surprised that the press hasn't come around to question you by now."

Shit, he hadn't thought of that. "Good point. I suppose they may find out and come around. What should we do?"

"In my opinion? The world is hunting for Sophie as we speak, including someone out there who wants her dead. They may have said they can't touch you in that alleyway, but who knows how powerful the person who set Sophie up is or what they're capable of doing. The press could find out where you are, so can these people. I think you should seriously consider calling Sergeant McKinnon and explain to him what happened, and that you found Sophie in that alley. Maybe let the authorities handle this."

"You know I can't do that. Death threats aside," Korban said, his hands starting to shake. "You know what they'll do to her. I wouldn't wish that on my worst enemy."

"As long as she is here and hidden away, it won't look good if the police do show up to question you. You could end up back in that facility, Korban, just as fast as she could."

"I'm not going back there, no way. Never again," He shook his head fervently. "I'm not letting them take Sophie to that place either."

"There is always a chance that they won't take Sophie there," RJ continued with equal persistence. "Her husband is wealthy. Knowing his team of company lawyers alone I'm sure they could prevent her from getting mistreated."

The glare Korban gave him must have made his point without words because his normally take-charge friend went very quiet *very* fast, and he even took a small step back. "Her husband could be the reason she is in this mess, RJ," Korban managed between gritting his teeth. "Who knows if that was his plan all along? She told me the first night we met he was cheating. Maybe this was some elaborate scheme to bump Sophie off so he could be free to roam as he pleased."

"We don't know that. Not for sure," RJ held up his hands diplomatically. "After tomorrow night, once you and her both are calmed down we can take a look into this. Until then we have to keep a low profile, and if the police or press do show up... just lay low."

"She should be fine in your room," Alex finally spoke up after being so quiet, which was extremely rare for him. "As long as they don't happen to have a search warrant ready to go. Or probable cause when they come knocking on our door."

RJ nodded grimly. Korban sighed. "Look, right now I know this isn't much of a plan. We're all winging this and it's frustrating. After the full moon we can regroup and actually make something more tangible to follow, but in the meantime..." He trailed off, uncertain of what more to say on it.

"In the meantime," RJ cleared his throat, regaining his composure once more, "I think that it's a good idea for you and Sophie to get a bit of air. Let's go clean up the garage in case we have any unexpected guests."

Alex nodded in agreement, and they parted ways. Once the

coast was clear, Korban returned back to his bedroom door, knocking lightly on it. He heard her inhale in scent and his heart skipped a beat when her voice came, "Come in."

He opened the door and peered inside. She was wearing one of his shirts and a pair of his gray sweatpants, and looked just as breathtaking as the first night he laid eyes on her at the bar. If not even more beautiful, her blue eyes already half-turned to bright gold. She gave him half a smile, her cheeks going pink. "You know, it's getting harder to ignore your reaction to me now that I can smell you."

Korban couldn't help but give her a flirty wink. "Funny, I was about to say the same thing to you."

Her eyes glistened and a full smile spread across her face. "I borrowed some clothes for now. I hope it's okay."

It was his turn to blush, and he nodded as his cheeks went hot. *Stupid, Korban. Be cool.* "Of course." She needed something to wear that wasn't stained in her own blood, but for a moment his brain stuck on the idea that she was wearing his clothes. Right now she seemed really eager to get out of that room, if only for a little while. He completely understood the feeling. He opened the door and gestured with his hand, like the valets did in old movies. "Right this way, ma'am."

Sophie anxiously stepped towards the door but hesitated when she reached his side. An unreadable expression crossed her face and she suddenly reached and took his hand. He felt her tension, her nerves on edge. This close her scent told him so much. She was afraid to run into Alex or RJ, afraid she would harm one of them or someone else on the way outside. By touching him she was trusting him, to not only keep her away from others but to protect her as well.

He guided her through the apartment. Though she tensed the

moment she caught RJ and Alex's scents, so fresh in the kitchen, it only took a squeeze of her hand to regain her composure. He lead her up the small flight of stairs that went up to the roof.

The instant they were outside he felt the tension leave her, just as it left him. He gave her a smile and she returned it. They made their way over to where a trio of plastic lawn chairs were placed. "The three of us come out here a lot, and just sit and relax."

Her nostrils were flaring, inhaling the air around them. Her eyes widened in surprise and he understood. Around the two of them were their own scents, and the ingrained smells of sweat, beer, and laughter. Then a breeze picked up the scents of the city were added to the mix. The steel, stone and earthy scent mixed with exhaust and age that rolled off the buildings; the fishy smell of the lake, the pungent aroma from the various dumpsters and trash cans; the wonderful blend of restaurants and greasy fast food. There were millions of different scents, some very new to Sophie. Even the once unpleasant smells held a certain curious sensation and were not as overwhelming as they were interesting.

Then there was the view. Though it had always been fairly impressive to his human eyes, to see the glittering lights of the hospitals and the white glow of the dome on the horizon, there was even more to be seen through the wolf's eyes. Every texture was sharp, every brick in the surrounding buildings easy to see and even in the moonlight everything was as clear as day. Not quite as keen as when the sun was out, but there was a remarkable ease of seeing everything without the need of a light. The moon hung in the sky, swollen and bright, tearing their gaze away from all the hustle and bustle on the earth below. The stars almost seemed to dance around the glowing orb, spiraling galaxies and thousands of stars visible even through the hazy glow of the city.

The sounds of the city were almost like music up here, a fitting companion to the entrancing light show above. The roar of car engines soaring along the highway, the gurgle of water rushing in the sewers, the lapping of waves on the lake, the heartbeats of passing strangers, the constant hum of electricity behind it all keeping the rhythm of the city. This close to the full moon the sounds were a symphony, a constant and mesmerizing beat.

"Amazing," Sophie's voice came out as a breathy whisper. "So this is how you see the world... it's incredible."

"It gets better in time. Your body adapts, things aren't so overwhelming. It takes time, like most things do." He nodded, watching her expression as she took it all in. He didn't want to ruin this moment for her but the distant wail of sirens reminded him of the danger she was still in. "There's things you need to know, Sophie. Things they don't report on the news."

She turned to him and gave him a questioning look. "What else do I need to know about all this?"

He wished he didn't have to tell her this, but she needed to be warned. "They told me at the... hospital... that there are a couple common outcomes after you are attacked by a werewolf. Most people die from the initial attack, the wounds being too severe and the blood loss too much to recover from. Then there are ones like me, who survive and become werewolves as well. But there's also the possibility of not surviving the transformation." He pauses. "After seeing you attacked on a night when there was no full moon I wonder if there is also a possibility of turning and not going back..."

Her eyes widened and watered a little in surprise, and her lips pursed with worry at the grim news. "So I'm not exactly in the clear, am I?"

He nodded, and she wrapped her arms around herself. He had the urge to wrap his arms around her, to comfort her, but he hesitated, giving her space and time to digest this. She stared up at the moon silently for a few more minutes, then sighed in acceptance. "So there's another reason I shouldn't go running back home... I might not even survive through tomorrow night. I could go home and Danny would see I'm okay, only to..." She trailed off.

Korban gave a small nod. "I'm sorry I didn't tell you before. I thought you should know, before..."

Sophie turned to him again, her eyes seemed to turn a brighter yellow out here in the moonlight. "Thank you, for being honest with me. Even when the truth hurts," she shivered and this time he moved closer, and she leaned against him. "If this is my last night alive, I wish more than anything that I could be with my son. Not everyone gets the chance to say good bye... if only I could hold him once more and tell him everything he needs to know."

She paused, and he seized the moment and blurted, "The only thing he really needs to know is that you love him," he rambled on quickly, "I mean, I know that sounds really cheesy, like something from a Hallmark card, but it's true."

Sophie pulled away to look at him and she smiled, even though her eyes were still glistening with unshed tears. "If this really is my last night before the end, then other than being with my son, I can't think of a better place to be than here with you."

His heart gave a happy flutter at that, which only continued when she rested her head against his shoulder and stared up at the moon above. "I've lost touch with all my other friends through the past few years. The only real friend I've had through this time was my sister, and even she hasn't been around as much lately because of her career starting to take off. Out of all of my friends, though, I've never felt this level of trust before, or this comfort. You make me feel safe, even if... even if I don't make it."

He put his arm around her when she began shivering again,

and he felt a drop of water land upon his warm skin. He couldn't let her give up hope, not now, not ever. "I promise you Sophie, whatever it takes, I will help get you through this alive."

She slid her arms around him and her shivering subsided as she snuggled into his embrace. "I know you'll try your best. Don't blame yourself if-"

"Shhh," Korban put his finger to her lips and her cheeks went pink. "Don't say it." For a moment he regretted telling her the news, but he knew that she didn't need another man in her life who was deceiving her.

The sirens in the distance were as sharp and clear as if the police car was right on their street. She gave a heavy sigh. "I guess that's our cue to go back inside." Sophie's eyes glistened as they met his once more. "Thank you for bringing me up here. I hope we can do this again, maybe under better circumstances."

Korban's heart swelled at that and he nodded. "I'd like that." He opened the door for her, then made a graceful sweeping gesture with his hand. "After you, madam."

~*~

"Mommy!" Daniel's voice was filled with laughter as he rushed ahead of her through the green, neatly clipped grass. "Catch me, Mommy!"

"Danny, not so fast!" She was chasing after him, trying to catch up to him. She knew this place as well as he did, a sprawling green field near Daniel's favorite playground where they had spent hours together. "Don't go too far away!"

His laughter came again as he darted behind a tree on the edge of the field. The sun was shining and the flowers blooming, the scent filling the air, along with Daniel's, which she followed behind the tree, panting, "Danny, come on, let's get back to-" He wasn't there, behind the tree, and his scent was gone again. "Danny!" She glanced around the thick trunk, not finding him there or up the tree. "Daniel, where are you?"

She heard his laughter again, floating on the wind, his scent there, and she ran again. "Mommy, Mommy, come and find me!"

She saw a blond head bobbing from the bushes, and she leapt after him. She ran as fast as she could to catch up to him, unnerved by his teasing playfulness when she was so desperate to get to him. "Danny!" She sprung through the bushes, cornering him. "Danny…"

"Mommy!" He called to her, even though she was standing there, though his playful lilt was gone. "Mommy? Mommy where are you?" He suddenly gasped, backing away, his eyes wide in horror as he stared at her. "N-nice… nice doggy…"

"Daniel…" It came out as a growl from her muzzle. She cried out but it didn't escape the curl of her lips, or the snap of her teeth. The wolf was in full control now, and her hackles rose. The small sobbing boy before her was nothing more than prey, smelling delectable with that fear rolling off of him, the wet thumping of his racing heart too irresistible.

She leapt for his throat, and Daniel screamed.

~*~

Sophie screamed and leapt up, thrashing at the covers. They were damp and clung to her skin, reeking of her sweat. Her nostrils flaring she glanced wildly around the dark bedroom. She was alone, but Korban's scent was there. Her hands were trembling and her throat was dry. She felt feverish and her bones ached. Glancing to the alarm clock on the nightstand, the glowing red numbers read three twenty-two in the morning, which meant she'd only been asleep for about two hours since her previous nightmare.

Too shaken to even attempt to sleep again, she got up and paced, until a cramp ripped through her stomach and made her cry out. She couldn't stand this, her entire body was aching and burning up, worse than any fever she'd run and more uncomfortable than any menstrual cycle she'd gone through. She spotted a bottle of water on the dresser and grabbed it, gulping it down in nearly one swig. The water itself felt as cold on her throat as if it had been sitting in the fridge, even if the bottle itself couldn't have been much less than room temperature.

Sweat still formed on her brow, and she felt suddenly too warm, even in the over-sized t-shirt and thin sweatpants she was borrowing. She needed air, feeling suddenly caged and claustrophobic. Moving over to the window she unhinged the lock and lifted it up. The cool spring air rushed in and she gulped it down, the cramps inside of her subsiding as she inhaled the blend of so many scents.

Gazing out at the night sky the moon shone brightly among thick clouds. Staring up at it, Sophie wondered how any of this was possible. So much had changed for her, her life as she knew it had ended just hours ago. She should have died in that alley, that monstrous wolf could have torn her apart. Yet miraculously Korban arrived to her rescue, and a new danger loomed around the corner. All brought upon by that glowing orb in the sky, which seemed more menacing than she ever remembered as she stared up at it now.

When she closed her eyes the scene from her dream flashed behind her eyelids, and suddenly the stuffy warmth of the room vanished as a cold chill ran through her. She wrapped her arms around herself and trembled. She missed Daniel more than anything and wanted to hold her son one more time. Yet she was too dangerous to be near him like this. If she smelled him and did the same thing to him as she did to Alex… she didn't want to think it. If she couldn't control herself the way Korban could, she wondered if it wouldn't be so bad if tonight when the moon was full she didn't make it to see the morning. Not that she didn't want to live, she just couldn't live with herself if she harmed anyone. Alex had been lucky.

And Korban... he didn't smell like prey, and didn't fear her. He definitely had a crush on her, the way his scent changed around her, when she spoke with him. She wasn't sure how to respond to that. There was just too much going on right now, the last thing on her mind was being intimate with another man. Maybe a part of her hoped this was just a dream, and she'd wake up and her life would be just as normal as it had ever been.

Another part of her knew though while this could be the end, and that her last night on earth could easily be spent in Korban's loving, welcoming arms. It wouldn't be such a bad way to spend her final hours. Yet her conscience got the best of her there, too. She couldn't do that to Korban. Even if he wanted it, she was afraid that if it really was her last night, to leave him after having an intense connection... it would break his heart. From what he'd told her, he had more than enough of his share of heartbreak. She wouldn't add to his pain and suffering. Not if she could help it.

Staring up at the moon, she glared at it in defiance. Her lower lip trembled a little but her gaze remained firm. She was afraid of many things at that moment, but she wouldn't let that floating orb in the sky rule her existence, or doom her to the grave. Her eyes raked over the city, wondering who was responsible for attacking her, and if they were having trouble sleeping over it. Her spiteful, bitter side hoped just as much as her good side that whoever it was had worse nightmares than her tonight.

As the pain began to flare up again, she clutched her stomach and crawled back into the bed. As she closed her eyes and attempted sleep through the growing pain, she had a very bad feeling that it was going to get worse before it got better.

9: TRANSFORMATION

Unfortunately, she was right.

She woke sometime later that day, the room bright from the sunlight pouring in, but she was in too much pain to contemplate the time. She didn't care what time it was, or about anything at that moment. All she wanted was for the pain to stop. It thrummed through her, from the very core of her being. Even her eyelids hurt.

Sweat poured from her body and her skin felt more on fire than any sunburn she'd ever experienced. There was a cool, blissful sensation of a cold, damp cloth being pressed to her forehead, but it was quickly warmed by her burning skin. "It's okay, Sophie. I'm here," Korban's worried voice floated in the air, but it hurt too much to open her eyes, and her teeth were gritting together to keep from screaming.

There was a cool plastic bottle pressed to her lips, and before she could even taste the water in it the bottle was empty. Even though she had sated her thirst just a second before, already her throat was dry. Nothing could sate her at that moment.

Sophie's mind felt torn in two, and she wondered if the pain was making her go mad. She could feel disjointed emotions and thoughts run through her mind. She wanted to run from Korban one moment, the next she wanted to tear off his clothes and either eat him, or fuck him. She was in too much pain to act on it, regardless of the intention.

Her chest rose and fell rapidly, panting as if she was running a marathon. Her body and mind were at war, the lycanthropy virus battling the last of her defenses. She felt another cool cloth warm against her forehead and she moaned as a fierce cramp ripped through her abdomen, causing her to curl in to herself. Her fingers found a pillow and gripped it until fabric ripped and fluffy cotton bulged through the seams. It did ease the ache in her hands and wrists, if only for a few precious moments.

At some point Korban lifted her and carried her from the room, telling her something but she couldn't hear over her pounding migraine, or maybe it was her heart echoing through her skull. This time when she caught the scent of two other men she didn't want to hunt them, instead she wanted to run and hide. She almost was able to struggle away from him until an agonizing shock rushed through her spine and this time she couldn't hold back the scream.

She doubled over and almost struck her head on the counter as they passed through the kitchen, but Korban managed to keep his balance and carried her down a flight of stairs to a cooler room with smaller windows and less light.

She was lowered onto a soft blanket that was draped over the cool concrete floor and she writhed upon it until his hand brushed her forehead again. As hot as his skin was, something about his touch calmed her, even if it didn't completely remove the ache. She caught his shirt with her fingers before he could move away, and managed to focus her gaze upon him. "Don't go," she managed to blurt before biting back another scream as another lightning bolt of pain coursed from her spine through the rest of her body.

He gazed down to her and nodded, relaxing alongside her. This close she saw the sheen of sweat over his skin, his owns muscles just as tense. He was in just as much pain as she was, and yet he was able to put aside his agony in order to help her deal with her own.

Korban took her hand and squeezed it tenderly, his other hand taking the corner of the blanket and wiping the sweat from her forehead. "It'll be okay," he spoke softly, the pain apparent in his voice. "I won't go anywhere. Alex will lock us down here for the night, I'll help you get out of your clothes so they don't get you tangled up when the moon rises if you can't do it yourself, okay?"

The thought of being naked in front of him would normally make her blush, but her face was already flushed from her blood burning up. She managed to nod, her teeth gritting together again as another wave of pain crashed through her. Korban stayed by her side but turned away, giving her privacy. She wouldn't let the pain take her dignity away, and clinging to that thought she managed to get out of the borrowed sweatpants and shirt easily. The cool air of the basement felt wonderful on her feverish skin, but she pulled the sheet over to cover up, then let her hand return to the side of Korban's arm, her fingers brushing against his skin and causing him to turn and gaze to her. His heart was racing in time with hers and his golden eyes were even brighter than before. He offered her his amazing smile, reaching over and caressing her cheek with his palm. "It's almost time." He studied her as if memorizing her like this, and a new anxiety began to fill her when she remembered his warning last night.

The shadows were growing in the room as the sun sank behind the cityscape. From the basement, where she figured they had to be, the sky outside of the small rectangular windows turned a pale lavender, then a deep blue violet.

Alex had locked the steel reinforced door from the outside and was safely upstairs, blasting his stereo and tinkering on one of his personal projects. They could hear the familiar twangy guitar of Creedence Clearwater Revival's *Bad Moon Rising* beginning and Korban rolled his eyes, which made a short, nervous bit of laughter escape from her.

Sophie's heart was pounding so hard, she thought it would burst from her chest at any moment. Her palms were sweaty, shaking. He took her hand and smiled. "It's going to be fine, Sophie. I'm here. Your Pack."

It was as if that one word filled her soul to the point of bursting. The moon was rising, like an enormous pearl glowing against the black velvet sky. She felt its rays scorch her skin, until even the muscles and bone beneath became hot, melting.

She screamed, the pain of her body burning up becoming too much. She felt something cool stir deep inside, cool and soft as a breeze in the night. Her aching bones and flesh stretched. Fingers broke as they morphed into solid, thick paws. Her spine arched as it sprouted bones, and a long tail extended. In a wave of wind over her throbbing body, soft golden fur sprouted from her red, burning flesh.

Her scream became a deeper, baying sound as her mouth became impossibly longer, her nose going wet and cold. Suddenly the thought of being lost in the night, to slip into the abyss instead of living in excruciating pain was more than welcome.

She saw Daniel, then Korban, and then was lost to the darkness.

~*~

Korban's eyes opened and he expected it to be morning, the sun streaming in, his body sore from the transformation once more. He lifted his head and gazed around, the room still in blue-gray hues. He never woke while transformed before, usually the memories of the previous night more like scattered images, nothing ever this tangible. His heart thrummed against his ribcage, adrenaline rushing through his veins and subduing any remnants of pain. He stretched, the feeling of being on all fours with no pressure on his knees or back strangely comfortable.

He could see the full moon hanging in the sky and for a moment he was drawn to it, until the faint howls rang through the city and caught his attention. Tossing back his head he joined the chorus, until a louder and much closer growl stopped him, his hackles raising as he spun around, nearly tangling himself in his long, canine legs.

He lifted his gaze and there she was, his heart almost stopping. Her ears were back, her pale fur raised and her teeth bared. Her tail was tucked so tightly between her legs as she circled him that at first sight he wondered if she didn't have one like him. He sniffed the air, and could smell fear and anxiety rolling from her. Not that he needed to smell it, her eyes were bright and glaring suspiciously at him, her body tense and fur ruffled as she cautiously circled around him. He opened his mouth to speak to her, but no words came, only a soft whine that made her jump in surprise. He couldn't communicate with her like this, and so he had to use other signals to calm her down. He stood his ground and watched her, his eyes never leaving her as she moved along the corners of the room.

They danced in circles like this for countless minutes, until Sophie's wolf realized he wasn't going to pounce upon her or hurt her, and that was when her gaze changed from one of suspicion and threat to a cautious curiosity. She stopped circling around him and lifted her ears, sniffing him again, considering. Maybe even remembering him as human, as her scent was not too different in this form so he imagined the same was true for his own.

Her tail uncurled from between her legs as she slowly approached him. He remained still, keeping his head high, his gaze lowered to avoid confrontation. She padded around him, then hesitantly leaned in and sniffed the fur along his shoulder. His heart was racing, and he battled every instinct that told him to run, trying instead to focus on her feminine scent, which was pleasant and alluring. Her nose prodded his thick fur as she sniffed him, and the warm wet touch of her nose against his skin made him jump, causing her to leap away, eyes wide and round.

Something about her expression amused him and he wanted to laugh, but instead his jaw opened and a huffing sound emerged, his tail wagging. It was an odd yet familiar sensation. She tilted her head, then realizing his reaction flicked her ears in agitation before her own muzzle curved a little and her tail slowly wagged.

He felt suddenly so alive, invigorated by the energy of the full moon and her company. They romped like two big clumsy pups around the basement, nosing through so many different scents, things that made Sophie huff and growl. When they heard the howls through the city again the two of them tossed their heads back and bayed at the moon, until weariness set in near dawn and Korban curled upon the blanket on the floor, leaving her room to curl up freely if she liked. Even as he calmed down from their play, his heart sped up again as she lay next to him, snuggling against him and resting her head on her paws. He lay his head down tentatively over her and she tensed, then relaxed and melted against him.

Closing his eyes, he hoped that he would remember every detail when he woke.

~*~

Full moon nights were mandatory overnight shifts for everyone, and when the coffee finished brewing at ten-thirty Sergeant McKinnon was the first one there to refresh his mug. Ever since the public attack and disappearance of Sophie Bane the other night sleep had been scarce. Between the media hounds and the nonstop calls with "leads" for the case his once quiet department was working overtime. He returns to his desk after filling his mug and sips it, black and strong and exactly what he needs to jolt his senses. He had only been out maybe three minutes and already the ancient phone on his desk was blinking with new messages. Sighing he settles into his office chair and pushes the button.

There are three messages, one with a lead claiming they saw the rogue werewolf running along Erie Boulevard, another who swore they had a tip that Sophie was spotted shopping at Destiny USA… nothing he hadn't heard or not checked through the rumor mill. The third message claimed aliens took her. He was about to give up on any useful information that night when his cell phone blared to life. One of his officers, hopefully with some news. He snaps open his phone. "Tell me something good, Smith."

"We've been searching for Brett Kensington to question him, and tonight uh… we found something all right."

An icy chill courses through him, that gut feeling that told him things were bad before it was said. "His home was empty, but their cars were packed the other day according to neighbors. They hadn't responded to our calls so we checked out their lake house over in Liverpool." He pauses.

"You find him there?" Tim wasn't in the mood to be left in suspense.

"No, but their cars were there, unpacked. No answer when we knocked. Then I flash some light inside, 'cause it was dark… and there's a puddle of blood."

Tim nearly knocks his coffee over as he grabs a pen and paper. "Give me the address. Do not go in there, whatever you-"

Smith rattles off the address, then continues, "Sir, there's… *oh my God!*"

Tim bolts for the door, grabbing his keys and his jacket,

clutching the cell phone tight. There are incoherent shouts and shots fired. Tim yells to his partner next office down as he bursts into the hall, "Andy, get up, we're headin' out! Call for back up! Officer down!"

There is a loud scream, followed by vicious snarling and Tim shouts into the phone, "Hang on! We're on our way!"

~*~

Sophie woke up, her body stiff and sore. Sunlight streamed in through the basement window. She'd made it through the night. She was still herself. Korban had kept his word yet again.

It was so strange to come down from that high that came with the full moon. She could see, but felt blind compared to last night. Her other senses seemed muted as well, even though they had actually returned to normal. The only sense that still seemed stronger compared to usual was her sense of smell, and even this felt slightly stuffy compared to last night.

She stretched slowly, and became very aware of two things. One, she was completely naked. Secondly, Korban was spooning her from behind, also very naked.

Korban stirred beside her, stretching and loosening his embrace around her. Feeling suddenly shy, Sophie pulled away from the warm shelter of his arms, and covered herself with her hands. Unfazed, he yawned and smiled, blinking his brilliant yellow eyes open. "G'mornin'. Sleep well?"

"Yes actually, yeah I did." It was difficult to have a casual conversation when both parties were butt naked. "Do we... is there something I could cover up with?"

"Oh, yeah, of course," Korban quickly got up and Sophie turned away, her blush flaring crimson.

There was a rustle of cloth behind her and then a soft blanket was draped over her shoulders. "Th-thank you," she stammered, not looking in his direction just yet.

He chuckled, "Don't worry, I've covered up too." He sat down beside her, another blanket wrapped around his waist. "So how are you feeling this morning?"

"Different." She had a feeling her blush wasn't going anywhere anytime soon, especially since she secretly had enjoyed the view. She tried quickly to compose herself. *You've got to think about Danny. And if Lucas is innocent...*

Nikki's suggestion echoed in her mind. *You said he's a pretty-looking puppy, right? Why not use that to your advantage?*

Korban either played her embarrassment coolly or he was being a gentleman. "Yeah, it takes some getting used to. The transformation, and then the absence of all that power," he smiled to her. "The hard part is over though. You didn't give in to the wolf, at least not completely. Once you've let it know who's boss each full moon gets easier." He paused for a long moment then asked, "Do you remember anything from last night?"

She shook her head. "No. Just a lot of pain, then I passed out," it was her turn to pause, her eyes meeting his still amber ones. "Do you remember?"

"That's the funny thing, actually," he scratched the back of his head, frowning thoughtfully, "I do. I usually don't, but I can remember everything." He smiled to her in wonder. "It was amazing. Incredibly weird to move on four legs and howl at the moon. To see the night through the wolf's eyes."

She wished she could remember it, after all the pain it would be worth it to have some sort of unusual reward. Still, she was thankful that everything was less sensitive than the previous night regardless of what she couldn't remember. It was so quiet without the constant beating of her heart echoing in her head. The door suddenly opened and she was surprised that it sounded normal to her ears. For a second her heart sped up when Alex peered in, but she didn't feel the urge to pounce on him and rip out his throat when she caught his scent.

"Mornin' Sophie, mornin' Lobo... I hope you're hungry, though I bet the two of you worked up an appetite last night," Alex grinned mischievously from the top of the stairs.

"*You cooked?*" Korban exclaimed, and at her questioning look revealed, "Alex would burn toast without RJ's help if given the chance."

That Cheshire-cat grin only widened as he tentatively headed down into the basement, keeping close to the stairs and an arm behind his back. "I paid a professional baker to whip us up three dozen donuts, and a fresh batch of coffee."

He proudly held up the Dunkin Donuts bags with a dramatic flourish as he reaches the bottom of the stairs. Sophie couldn't help but giggle as Korban shook his head and went over to accept the bags filled with donuts, "I should have guessed."

"Hey, why cook when you can leave it to the professionals? I'll get you guys some clothes too. If you want them, that is," he wiggled his eyebrows suggestively and it was Korban's turn to turn scarlet. He playfully boxed with his friend for a moment, then Korban caught his arm and spun him around. "Ahh! Okay, okay, Uncle! I give bro!"

Korban laughed and let him go. Alex pouted and rubbed his arm, but the smile still glistened in his eyes. He glanced over to Sophie again as Korban returned to her side with the donuts and coffee. As much as her stomach was growling the coffee smelled wonderful, even if she normally preferred tea for breakfast. She accepted the warm Styrofoam cup and sipped it as Alex asked from where he stood by the stairs, "How are you feeling this morning, Sophie?"

She didn't answer until she tore into one of the glazed donuts, barely tasting the sugary confection as she swallowed a massive bite. "Better, I guess. I'm still not sure if I'll repeat… what happened before." Her blush continued to heat her cheeks, and surely her face would remain scarlet for the rest of the day at this rate.

"It's okay, I learned my lesson. I'll keep my distance," Alex chuckles. "If you guys need anything else at all, just let me know. I'll go see what we have in the attic as far as things you can wear, Sophie."

She wanted to say that wouldn't be necessary. She felt okay now, normal. Surely she could go home. Still, she remembered that there was more to this than being a werewolf. Someone had attempted to take her life, in a way that put an entire crowd of people in danger. If she did return to Lucas and Daniel now, even as strong as she was, they may attempt to finish her off again. And if Lucas, or worse, Danny got in the way… she couldn't do that to her family. As painful as it was to be away from her son and even to some extent her husband, she couldn't put them in danger. Not from herself or the one who was targeting her. "Thank you. I appreciate it."

"No problem," Alex said, giving a wave and heading back up to the apartment.

Losing count of how many donuts she inhaled, she gazed to Korban, who seemed even more content now that he had his morning coffee. "You made it," he said with a smile. "Now comes the hard part."

"Now we find out who set me up in the first place," Sophie likes how Korban's thoughts seem to reflect her own. His determination fuels her own. "Where do we start?" Though the moment the words left her she realized the most likely suspect, and a bit of anger and a lot of pain flashed across her expression. "Lucas..."

Korban nodded grimly. "As much as I know it hurts you, it's possible he could be behind it. Which is another reason why I was afraid to take you to the hospital that night."

Feeling suddenly cold she drew the blanket closer and wrapped her arms around herself. "He was cheating on me but I never thought he'd be capable of doing something this... horrific," she finally settled on a word, even if it didn't seem to be gruesome enough to cover everything she experienced.

"Do you know who he was seeing?" Korban hesitantly asked.

She shook her head. "That's the worst part. I only have things she left behind. Underwear and bras, or what was left of them. Empty condom wrappers in the trash." The raw pain and anger resurfaced, causing her to choke up. "In our bedroom, the bathroom, and even the car. I just don't know how he could do this to me. Cheating was bad enough, but if he... he did this to get me out of the picture, so that I couldn't even be a part of Danny's life, to never get a chance to watch him grow up..." She trailed off, tears filling her eyes. It hurt more now that she'd admitted it out loud.

When her tears blurred her vision she could smell his scent grow stronger, and knew he was there before his arms wrapped around her. She didn't resist him, sagging into his embrace. "If it was Lucas, he will pay."

She nodded, breathing his familiar scent in as he held her. His scent was already connected to so many memories, of their dance at the ball, him coming to her rescue, and now with him simply being there and comforting her. She suddenly pulled away, gazing up to Korban as an idea struck her like lightning. "Korban, if it wasn't

Lucas, maybe it was her. Whoever he's been seeing might have wanted me out of the way to have him to herself. Maybe there's a way to find out who she is with a bit of her scent. I'm sure it would be on one of those items. I kept them hidden in a shoebox in my closet, for the day I'd be brave enough to finally confront Lucas about it all."

"I think you're right. Whoever she is, she might know something. We have to find out who she is, and if she knows anything about the attack. Maybe there's a clue on one of those things you found that will point us in the right direction." Korban paused, studying her closely. "Are you sure you'll be okay with this?"

"It's not like I have much of a choice anymore," Sophie sighed in resignation. "Someone set me up. I want to know who. It could be my cheating husband or his mistress. Or maybe it's someone else entirely, but it's as good a place as any to start. So enough second guessing and worrying about how I feel. More than anything right now, I want to know who did this to me."

She was filled with a fierce strength, and even as sore as she was suddenly she felt ready to get up and start their search. Clutching the blanket she went to stand up, much to her pained body's protest. She grit her teeth together and was proud of herself for managing to stand despite her knees buckling. Korban stood with a fluid grace that seemed to even surprise him, and he offered her his hand. She managed a grimace. "Thanks, but if I don't learn to do it myself, sooner or later you'll get tired of waiting around on me."

His blush suddenly rivaled her own, his eyes sparkling when they met hers again. "I could never get tired of waiting on you," he said with a teasing smile. "Let's go upstairs and get dressed before the neighbors start talking."

She smirked at that, and though her steps were slow she maintained her balance as they headed for the stairs. "I'm sure after last night they aren't the only ones talking. I'm amazed that RJ and Alex were able to sleep at all last night from what you said. I really wish I could remember something."

"I wish you could too," he smiled, a distant look in his eyes. "It was amazing. I've never felt so free before."

Sophie watched his expression change from happy reminiscing to a more intense, serious look when his eyes regained their focus upon her. "I know you will be able to remember in time. You'll be able to control yourself much better now that the wolf is sated. If you ever feel yourself slipping away, I'll do whatever it takes to help bring you back. I promise."

~*~

His car is the first on the scene. The moment Sergeant McKinnon puts the squad car in park he is sprinting out of the vehicle, his hand at his pistol. He'd filled in Andy on the way over and his partner follows his lead, the pair alert and scanning the area with hawk-like eyes, taking in every detail. Andy Ellyk had been his partner for four years now, but they knew each other much longer than that. Even now they had a synchronicity that the older partners shared, the tall and lean, almost scare-crow like cop moving alongside him as if they'd practiced this before.

There was another squad car parked alongside the family caravan, and the small cabin appeared calm and quiet. It was a ranch style log cabin tucked in between a small clearing of evergreens and oak trees, the lake glistening and visible from where they stood. A very peaceful scene in the morning light, suddenly made eerie when he spies bullet holes in the bark of one of the nearby trees, and even more menacing massive paw prints in the dirt.

"Smith?" Andy calls out, glancing around.

They both pause to listen, stepping lightly and following the trail of paw prints as they wind around the side of the dark cabin. There was no response which meant Smith was either unable to respond or... he didn't want to think it. When he peers around the corner and sees a trail of fresh blood his heart sinks. The paw prints are disorganized here, the bright red blood still glistening in the dirt, splashed around like some macabre paint. There had clearly been a struggle and as Tim's eyes follow the madness he can almost picture it in his mind's eye. His eyes suddenly catch something familiar on the ground, splattered with mud and blood- a familiar police issued pistol. "Shit, Smith," he swears under his breath and continues to follow the bloody trail.

There are drag marks leading to the back porch, up the stairs. Where the hell was their back up? He begins to wonder as they carefully tread up the wooden stairs. Each creek of the steps made him wince, gripping his gun tighter.

The back screen door was torn open, the glass shattered and screen torn open wide, resembling a sharp series of jagged teeth and a gaping maw. To his growing horror the trail didn't stop outside, but continued into the dark cabin. "Jesus," Andy murmurs a prayer as they move forward. "We should wait for backup-" A low moan comes from inside the lake house, making both sergeants jerk their heads towards the sound.

Tim nods to Andy, the pair moving forward. Whoever was moaning inside suddenly gasped, as if waking abruptly and began to make choking sounds. Tim rushes forward, ducking in to the open screen door and heading towards the sound.

Inside the cabin dimly glistening in the morning sun there was even more blood. So much that it couldn't be all from one person. A teddy bear lay dripping on the ground, its black button eyes staring vacantly, a silent witness to this unspeakable horror. In the midst of this mess, something gold caught the morning sun and glistened. A police officer's badge, still attached to a swatch of blue fabric, mostly a dark red now.

The moaning came from behind them and Tim nearly jumps from his skin, whirling around.

A thin naked man is laying there, covered in blood and looking disoriented. "Wha… what happened? Who are you?" He blinks, seeing the blood around him and beginning to choke and gag again.

Tim lowers his gun, but keeps it at hand. "Who the hell are you?"

"Brett Kensington," the man confesses between gagging, covering his mouth and nose with his arm.

"Really, now…" He grabs his pair of silver handcuffs and approaches the man cautiously. "Don't move or my partner here will put a silver bullet in ya. Hands up."

The timid man chokes again, lifting his hands in the air slowly. "What… where's my wife? The kids…" He is shaking as Tim grabs his hands and snaps on the cuffs. The man gives a loud yelp as the silver touches his skin.

Tim growls under his breath. "I think you know, you stupid bastard," he pulls Kensington to his feet and shoves him forward. "Let's go. You're under arrest."

The man sputters, "What about my Miranda rights? You can't just-"

Tim tightens the cuffs and the man howls in pain. "Sorry pal, those are *human* rights. And according to law now, you're no longer human and up shit creek without a paddle."

~*~

After finishing breakfast and getting dressed they gathered around the kitchen table. Sophie kept her distance from his two human roommates. Korban watched her movements, still calculated and a bit stiff, and could hear the rush of her pulse. He wasn't sure if it was because she was just being overly cautious at the moment or if it was her nerves. After all, they were in the middle of discussing breaking and entering her home. RJ's frown kept growing with every passing moment.

Alex, on the other hand, was grinning eagerly. "So finally we get to plan an undercover mission! I haven't been this stoked since plotting our Senior prank."

This did nothing to improve RJ's mood. "Hopefully this will go over much better than that. Considering most of us were caught and nearly expelled."

"They never would have kicked you out, Golden Boy," Alex waved his hand. "Anyway, I have a few ideas. Sophie is obviously familiar with the area, so maybe she can lay it out for us. Then we can plan our attack from there."

Sophie gazed down and it was Korban's turn to frown. "Look Alex I know you want to help but please try to be considerate. This is Sophie's home we're talking about, not just some place she's familiar with."

Alex's expression turned serious, which startled him. "I know that, but it's also a dangerous place for her to be now. If they find out she survived that attack, our element of surprise will be gone and put us at a grave disadvantage, no pun intended. Whoever did set her up must have powerful means to an end, and we don't want to see what else they could be capable of if they find out their first plan failed."

Even RJ's jaw had dropped open. "Sometimes you really surprise me," Korban blurted and flashed him an impressed smile.

Alex beamed but it was brief. "Watching a lot of action movies pays off. Anyway, we have someone who knows the area very well. We just need a good time so that you two won't get caught sneaking around in there so you can be in and out." His tone softened when he gazed to Sophie. "I'm sorry you have to do this. Right now, though, your home is not safe. And there is always the possibility that someone who is within those walls is the brains behind your attack."

"It's okay," Sophie glances to Alex, careful not to meet his eyes. "I want to find out who did this, and my home is where we have to start looking for answers. Lucas is at the office all day, and Danny," a pained expression spread across her face, "he's in school. It would probably be best to go in before lunchtime in case he has a half day."

"Would anyone else be there during the day?" Alex asked.

Sophie thought for a moment, then said, "No one but the cleaning crew, and they only come two, maybe three times a week."

Alex's grin widened. "Perfect. I think I have just the plan."

10: HEIST

The three man crew pushed the cleaning cart into the elevator at precisely 9:59am, just as the microwave bell rang from the doorman's break room. The buttery scent of popcorn summoned the elderly man from his duty as record keeper of the comings and goings in the high profile condominium. A stylish and modern building that was owned by Bane Corporation and served the wealthy elite who didn't care to commute from their larger homes on the outskirts of the city.

He barely paid attention to the familiar uniforms that pushed the cart of mops and brooms past him and towards the elevators. After all, it was a rerun of fight week on *Jerry Springer*, and he reeked of anticipation- he couldn't wait to see the havoc break loose from the safety of the glowing television screen.

After glancing around the hall, a delicate hand pressed the button for the top floor. The Bane family's suite. When the elevator announced its arrival with a cheerful ding, the doorman didn't even glance up from the audience on screen, chanting for its familiar host.

The solid doors closed with a soft shudder, then the elevator lifted up, up...

None of the three spoke. When the elevator jerked to a halt, they held their breath... the doors opened with a soft exhale, revealing an elegant but empty corridor. The coast was clear and they remembered to breathe again.

Sophie, her blonde hair pulled up under a cap and eyes hidden behind thick prop glasses, nodded and lead the way to the front door of her home. Her delicate hand quickly entered the keypad's code and the lock clicked. She sucked in a deep breath and opened the door.

Her home was exactly as she'd left it, only empty and quiet. Sure, the same furniture was there, the vases filled with flowers and the large entertainment center; but it held no life, just a huge emptiness. She stepped in, slowly walking around.

Lucas and Daniel's scents were there, hanging heavily in the air and filled with pain and sorrow. She felt choked up and stopped in her tracks.

Alex glanced silently to Korban, who went over and touched her shoulder gently. She turned to him, her eyes glistening gold and emerald behind those comically thick plastic lenses. "You okay?" He asked softly.

She hesitated, but then gave a quick nod. "I'll be fine, it's just very strange sneaking into my own home and... feeling the energy here now."

Korban nodded in understanding. Heightened sense of smell, touch, sight, and sound weren't the only senses enhanced by lycanthropy. He could also feel the lingering grief and wondered if Lucas might be innocent after all.

They continued forward, Sophie leading them down the posh hall to a stylish office the size of their living room and kitchen back at the garage. A sleek, solid desk with the latest computer and a leather swivel chair was in the center of the room, surrounded by solid steel filing cabinets and book shelves that matched the desk. "I don't know what you might find in here, but it's worth a look. I'll go and get the shoebox in the bedroom," Sophie said quietly, her voice barely above a whisper.

Alex immediately went to the file cabinets, while Korban checked the desk drawers, fishing for any records that might enlighten them to Lucas' involvement, or his innocence. Tax records, financial records, investments; but nothing suspicious. They continued on to the second set of cabinets.

Sophie was about to leave the room, when a glint caught her eye. Going over to Lucas's desk, she gazed at the usually immaculate surface of her husband's desk. Here she froze, surprised... there was an old but clean frame, well maintained, sitting there. It held within it a picture of when she was younger, not too long after she had first met Lucas. She stared at her younger, happier self clinging to the arm of the devilishly handsome younger Lucas. He seemed much younger there; more carefree than he would be in the years that came after they married.

She hadn't seen the picture in so long she'd almost forgotten about it. The frame was polished metal, but there were flecks of something on the glass over the picture that smelled faintly of salt. She picked it up for a closer look, but yelped suddenly and dropped the frame back onto the desk in surprise. She glanced at her delicate fingertips and saw they were red, as if the frame had burned her like fire.

Korban rushed to her side, abandoning the cabinet full of tax records he'd been perusing for clues. "You alright?"

She shook her head, then it dawned on her. The frame was silver. "I guess that was pretty stupid of me to forget," she clenched her teeth in pain.

Korban glanced to Alex. "Keep searching, I'll make sure Sophie gets that silver burn taken care of." Alex nodded and carefully continued his search through another set of files.

He ushered Sophie into the bathroom, which they'd passed on the way to the office. He turned the faucet on and ran the water cold. "Here. It'll ease the pain for a moment and get any trace of silver off the burn."

She grit her teeth and stuck her fingers under the faucet, biting her bottom lip hard to stifle a scream. After a moment, though, the water eased the pain and the tension melted away from her body. "Luckily that frame was only silver coated, not pure," Korban reported, watching the water flow over her aching fingertips. His amber eyes met hers. "You okay?"

Forcing a smile, she nodded. "It doesn't hurt that much anymore."

~*~

Tim stared down at the man sitting across the table from him and his partner and wondered what this guy had to be thinking. This thin, balding man who cowered before them now, his small wrists blistered and red as if sunburned by the silver handcuffs. Korban had tipped him off, claiming this scrap of a man was looking to be bitten. Brett Kensington, just an average cog in the clock for a decent corporation, with an above average salary. He remembers the shattered family photograph, the smiling faces stained with blood at the scene. The bloody, dripping teddy bear. What had this man been thinking?

Brett Kensington was clearly distraught now, his lower lip trembling, a mad look in his haunted eyes. As many times as he did this, it never got easier. He studied the man before him who had it better than most, and wondered why he threw it all away. It never ceased to amaze Tim how normal all blood thirsty criminals looked, even ones who were actual monsters.

Andy cleared his throat. "You're lucky we were the first on scene. Not all of us take a chance to speak with monsters."

Brett hung his head dejectedly. "I want to speak with my lawyer."

They'd been doing this dance for over three hours. The long night was now becoming an even longer day. Andy was not as patient as Tim, but both of their tempers were wearing thin. He grit his teeth, which Tim knew was his way of counting down to keep his temper at bay. Before he could speak, Tim slapped his palms on the table, causing the frail werewolf before them to jump in sync with his partner. "We've already told you, no lawyer is even going to look your way, retainer or not. There are no rights for monsters," Tim paused, meeting the cowardly man's eyes. "However. If you start acting like a man and start talkin', maybe we can start treatin' you like a human."

Brett met his gaze for a long moment, his mouth drawn thin. Tim could see it easily though, the moment the walls were caving in. Suddenly the monster before them had very large, moist eyes. He broke his stare, hanging his head down as tears began to trail down his cheeks. "It wasn't supposed to be like this! They said it would be okay, it'd be fine after a few full moons. I'd be in control. They even gave me a drug, this serum to help with the transition, but all that did was make me black out and wake up in a dumpster."

"A dumpster where?" Tim asked, his heart racing as his cop instincts began to kick in. They were finally getting somewhere.

"The Rescue Mission on Adams, not far from the Oncenter. I was supposed to be there for a charity ball and instead I wake up in a dumpster with the worst hangover I've ever had. I guess the serum didn't mix with alcohol or something."

"Or something," Andy repeated, exchanging a glance with Tim. He wasn't the only one suspicious about this story.

"What happened when you woke up, Brett?" Tim asks, closely gaging the man's reaction.

As he predicted the man hesitates, blinking a moment, shifting his gaze away. "What do you mean, what happened? I woke up, got out of the dumpster, and got screamed at by my wife for the rest of the day for abandoning her at the ball."

"Hold on just a second. Back up. Earlier you said you were 'supposed' to be at the ball... assuming you hadn't gotten there. Now you're saying you ditched your wife there and got an earful?" Andy leans in, nostrils flaring as he stares the cowering man down.

"Ellyk..." Tim cautions, but Brett only tenses under Andy's stare, then continues to cower. Which makes Tim relax some, but not completely. This news was definitely relevant to more than one case. This could be the break they needed.

"Look, I didn't want any trouble. I don't remember what happened after I blacked out. I just..." Brett trailed a moment, then shook his head. "One minute I was fine. The band was playing a little too loud. I went upstairs, out for some air. Then," Brett pauses, worrying his lower lip, "I'm waking up, hurting everywhere, in a dumpster covered in filth and trash. And I see-" He stops, rather suddenly. "No. I'm not saying another word without my lawyer."

"We've already told you-!" Tim begins, but Andy is the one to yank the silver cuffs, causing the man to howl out in pain.

"I'm sick of the games, Kensington. What did you see? You see the mangled corpse of Sophie Bane there? You see her there, half eaten next to you? The blood and bones of some innocent woman making your den for the night? Or maybe you see nothing huh? Nothing but blood all around, no body left behind, just like your two kids and wife at the cabin by the lake?"

"No!" Brett yelps again, his face going pale. "No I didn't! I couldn't! My kids… Brenda…" His eyes well up again.

"Tell us what you saw, Kensington. Or I'm going to assume the worst, and that means," Andy pulls out his pistol, the bullet clicking into place in the chamber, "I don't hesitate to end my shift by ending you with a silver bullet in your brain."

The mousy man- an odd comparison, considering what he was- suddenly folds. "No, no, no! They can't be dead! I would never! I could never! I was supposed to be locked in and safe. It was supposed to be manageable!" His eyes widen, watery and huge behind his crooked spectacles. "I would never hurt my family or anyone. I blacked out. I couldn't control it. It wasn't me! It was the monster! You have to believe me. I love my family. I just wanted to be stronger."

"And where's all that strength gotten you, Kensington?" Tim crosses his arms over his chest, then repeats rather flatly. "What was in the dumpster with you, when you woke up?"

"I told you, I couldn't remember how I got there, or how it got their either!"

Andy puts a slight pressure on the trigger. "You think I'm kidding? You think we have time for games?"

"Wa-*wait!*" Brett yelps. Of course such a cowardly man would plead for his life. Tim wondered how long this man's family begged for their lives in vain. "I told you I swear I didn't do it." Andy cocks the gun as the man spills his guts, figuratively speaking. "There was this rag, this bloody rag, and it reeked of the stuff… it had a weird smell to it, almost like piss. Fear." His nose wrinkles at the memory.

"But I swear I didn't do anything! It was just there when I woke up!"

Tim's frown deepens. He wondered what else was in that dumpster. If they were lucky the trash would still be there. He pulls his cell phone from his pocket and speed dials waste management as his partner rests his gun and glares at their suspect. "There, was that so hard?"

The man sags his shoulders and gives them a pleading look. "Now can I call my lawyer? Or my wife? I need to find out if she's okay."

Andy's lip twitches, but Tim reaches over and puts a hand on his partner's shoulder. "Give him his phone call. If there is a chance that wasn't them in that cabin…"

Andy nods, and the receptionist for waste management picks up, greeting him warmly on the other line. Tim gets up and leaves the room. The operator that connected to dispatch was able to stop the truck on route.

The next hour went by in a flash. No one answered the first call, or the fourth of the fifth. It wasn't looking good for him, and it began to look worse as they locked him up in the jail and headed to the crime scene.

Ducking under the yellow caution tape, there was a deepening sense of wrongness as Tim approached the rather average looking green, rust-speckled dumpster. Unfortunately the evidence within the worn trash receptacle was not good for Kensington.

A blood soaked, torn piece of fabric was there as he said. What little splotches of the satiny fabric remained untarnished were a vivid white. The same color Sophie Bane had last worn on that fateful night.

~*~

While Korban tended to Sophie's wounded fingers, Alex carefully opened another filing cabinet and began shuffling through the thick files. The top two drawers were mostly certificates, property documents, deeds, income tax forms; nothing that would point towards a nefarious plot outside of tax evasion.

The third drawer held nothing of particular interest either, so he moved to the last cabinet. Just when it seemed there was nothing of interest in the final cabinet, something caught his attention- rather the absence of something. Wedged between various business documents was an unlabeled folder that was stamped with the Bane Corporation logo.

Strange, he thought. All of the other files, even the insignificant ones, had been marked and organized, except for this one. Pulling it free from the others, he flipped open the file to glance it over-

His cell phone exploded to life, and he jumped in surprise, the papers scattering as the file fell to the floor. Cursing under his breath, Alex fumbled in his pockets and retrieved his phone.

It was RJ.

"Damn man, you scared the-"

"Alex, you guys have to get out of there. The real cleaning crew just pulled up."

He swore and balanced the phone between his ear and shoulder as he bent down and quickly scrambled to get all the papers back in the folder. "We'll be right down RJ," he straightened up the papers and from between the pages a photo fell on the floor.

He picked it up and his heart nearly stopped when his brain made sense of the picture. "Don't worry, we're leaving *now*." Before RJ could reply, he hung up his phone. With the file in hand, he hurried up the hall and followed the sound of water and voices to the bathroom. "Lobo, Sophie- we have to leave now. The real crew is about to confuse the hell out of security if he looks up during a commercial break."

"Shit," Korban glanced up from tending Sophie's hand to the file in Alex's arms. "Find anything?"

"Something huge, I think," Alex glanced nervously to their exit. "We need to go. Now."

Sophie caught a whiff of Alex's fear and pulled her hand from the faucet, quickly turning it off with her good hand. They hurried quickly from the room, Alex stuffing the folder underneath his jumpsuit and Korban grabbing the cart in the hall, pushing it towards the elevator as Sophie reset the alarm and quickly hurried over to where they waited by the elevator. She grabbed a washcloth from the cart and wrapped it around her wounded hand that still stung from her silver burn, making a make-shift bandage out of the rag. Alex pushed the button, but to their horror the elevator was already descending to pick up the real cleaning crew.

The elevator had paused at the lobby floor and then began its ascent back up. She glanced over to the stair well. "Hurry, this way," she told the two of them, pushing open the door leading to the emergency exit stairs. Korban shoved the cart into the landing, abandoning it there as the three of them hurried down the stairs.

Sophie froze as the realization struck her only a few steps down. "The shoebox!" She turned to Korban, eyes wide.

Before Korban could say a word, Alex blurted, "Whoever Lucas is sleeping with isn't as important as what's in here," he gestured to the file, the manila corner peeking from his jumpsuit. "We have to get out of here, before we're caught with this. Trust me."

Reluctant but feeling the urgency rolling off Alex, she reluctantly nodded and the three continued their path to the ground level.

They managed to get down a few flights when they heard voices from a couple floors below them. The smell of oil, rank garbage, bologna sandwiches, sweat and beer- two maintenance men on lunch break. Sophie silently motioned for them to open the door on this floor, and they quietly slid the door open, then closed it again behind them. Thankfully, the hall on this floor was empty. They hurried to the elevator, holding their breath collectively as the light signaled the elevator's arrival on the floor they were on... then ascending further, towards the Bane condo.

They waited until the elevator reached its arrival on the top floor, then a few long moments afterwards Sophie hit the button for the elevator to come back down to their floor. All three of their hearts were racing as the elevator announced its arrival, then the doors opened. The elevator was empty and they quickly boarded it. To be on the safe side, Sophie hit the button for the third floor instead of the lobby, and they silently unloaded there and quickly finished their escape using the stairs.

Right as they reached the door to the lobby, Korban froze, listening beyond the door. The guard still appeared blissfully unaware of anything wrong, chuckling as the crowd jeered on the television. Just in case Sophie led them up the back hall towards a door that was obviously not used by the residents.

Rushing out of the back service door, a wave of exhilaration swept over the three of them. They ran up the alley to the rendezvous point and quickly scrambled into the car where RJ was anxiously awaiting. His heart pounding, Korban glanced behind them as the car eased into afternoon traffic, but they weren't being followed. At least for the moment.

Sophie panted beside him in the backseat, her face flushed from running and her emerald eyes bright, the golden flecks more brilliant. She couldn't help but smile to him. "We did it!" She turned to Alex. "What did you find?"

"I think we stumbled onto something huge," Alex pulled the file from his jumpsuit, handing it over to RJ when they stopped at a red light. "Check out the photos in there. I just hope I didn't see what I thought I saw."

RJ flipped open the folder, Korban and Sophie both peering over the backseat. Sophie's jaw dropped open, eyes wide and shrinking back instinctively. "No!" she gasped in disbelief.

The picture was of a monstrously huge wolf. Those hauntingly familiar, vicious eyes that were engrained on her brain, the same sharp teeth that tore into her- she wrapped her arms around herself and drew back into the seat. For a moment the images of the night flashed through her brain all over again, the rain of broken glass and the shouts, the beast lunging directly at her and grabbing her away, her husband screaming at their bodyguards to not shoot- and suddenly the picture became very clear, and at the same time she went numb all over. "Lucas…"

11: EVIDENCE

The ride back to the garage was a silent one. Korban spent the remainder of their trip watching Sophie, who had drawn into herself and watched the scenery pass by. He couldn't bring himself to even glance at the folder until they returned to the safety of their apartment.

They gathered around the kitchen table, and though Sophie's nose wrinkled at the closeness of Alex and RJ, she didn't make any attempts to lunge for either of his roommates. Her human half was in full control at the moment. The painful truth was tucked between the thin pieces of cardstock lying in front of them. RJ glanced to Sophie and asked her, "Are you sure you're ready for this?"

She merely gave a sharp nod, and says, "No one ever says the truth comes easy," and flips the folder open.

Inside the file there were a few innocent seeming sheets of paper, stapled together and labelled as a copy of a police report. Attached to the slender packet by a normal paperclip was an image that was anything but normal- the familiar, monstrous and shaggy brown beast. The creature that had targeted Sophie, caught on security footage just before the attack that would change her life. A chill ran through Korban as Sophie stared at the picture again in disbelief. "That's the one," Korban managed to find his voice. "That's the werewolf who bit Sophie."

She stares down at the image, grainy and time-stamped but clear enough to evoke memories. The beast's eyes seemed even more blood red in the print out, and she reached out and pulls the picture free from the paperclip to study it closer. Her eyes narrow as she looks at the blurry image of the wolf, as though trying to understand its motives just from the photo.

RJ pulled over the notes and scanned them, his frown deepening. "Looks like Lucas has information on this werewolf. Apparently Bane Corporation runs a facility that is helping hold the recently infected to help them 'transition'. Sounds a lot like where they kept you after your attack, Korban."

An even colder feeling coursed through him and he had to suppress a growl, "What else does it say?" If he wasn't suddenly seeing red, he probably would have read it over himself.

RJ was quietly frowning again as his eyes raked over the pages, flipping through them. He froze and tensed when he reached the last page. Korban follows his friend's gaze to a yellow sticky note that was affixed to the final page of the packet, notes scrawled on it. Sophie went very still, though she couldn't hide the pain in her eyes. RJ rubbed his temples. "There's a few notes but that's all. Not sure what they mean."

"Let me see," Korban said with a growl that wasn't meant for RJ, though his friend didn't hesitate to quickly turn the paper over to him.

There were mostly numbers scratched down and a couple words, written neatly by someone's calculated hand. A small list that seemed to fill Sophie with more dread than the photographs in the folder, most likely because she knew exactly who wrote it.

8:45pm

8:58pm

2/27

B. Kensington

Lycanthrope infected?

Sophie gives a growl that makes Alex and RJ jump. "That first time listed, that was the time Lucas and I were to be on stage. The second time listed... that has to be about the time I was attacked," she frowns at the third set of numbers. "I am not sure what that date represents, if that is what it is... or who B. Kensington is, but I do know one thing and that is my husband's hand writing."

There was something awfully familiar about that name, but Korban couldn't place it. He looked to Sophie worriedly, "I'm so sorry Sophie-"

"Don't apologize," she shakes her head at him, "it's not your fault. None of this is." She wrung her hands together anxiously, gazing down at the evidence laid upon the table. "I knew it when I saw that picture in the car. Lucas did this. This is all his fault." Her hands were trembling and she suddenly stood up.

Korban got up too, but she shrugged away from him. "Please... I just need some time alone."

His heart broke a little as he caught the salty scent of her tears as she raced to his bedroom, slamming the door behind her.

~*~

There wasn't much time left on this world for Brett Kensington. The evidence only continued to mount up against him, which was good to close a case but this case would never see a trial by jury. There was only showing the proof to a judge who would weigh in more than likely with a guilty verdict. After all, Brett had gone out looking to become a monster and exceeded his expectations.

The paper bag was soaked with blood from the remnant found in the dumpster. Evidence, perhaps all they would ever find of Sophie Bane. There was even less left of Officers Smith and Wade, and the Kensington family. The blood splatter at the cabin was already being analyzed and more than likely would result in more grim discoveries.

The doors opened and a weary looking Lucas Bane walked in with two bodyguards flanking him. His dark Italian suit was clean and pressed, but even darker circles lined his eyes, an anxious look in his eyes. More than likely right now he was the only other man in the city who had fewer hours of sleep than they did. "You called, Officers?" He goes straight to business as he approaches Tim.

"Sergeant McKinnon and this is my partner Sergeant Ellyk," the exchanged firm handshakes, "and yes, I wanted to get you in right away. I'm afraid there's no easy way to say this. We found evidence less than a hour ago of your wife's attack and it's not good."

The notoriously cool businessman's face fell. "What... what did you find?"

Tim can see the man is struggling to keep his cool. Andy, who was more blunt, delivered the news as gently as he could. "We found a scrap of your wife's dress thanks to a confession of a werewolf we now have in custody. It doesn't look good, Mr. Bane. We are still investigating but so far this is the greatest lead we have gotten."

Lucas nods, quiet for a moment. Tim could see the wheels spinning as the man gathered up his thoughts. "So you have the... creature... in custody?"

Both sergeants gave a nod. This seemed to make Lucas relax then tense, his shoulders sagging then straightening again. "I'm glad the beast is off the streets. No one else should suffer like this," he trails off, then looks Tim in the eye. "Can I see this monster?"

"I don't know if..." Tim begins, but then reconsiders midsentence. "Okay, but it'll be with him behind bars. It's best for everyone that way."

Lucas nods in agreement.

They walk over to the window and Andy opens the blinds. Lucas' breath hitches a moment, his expression turning flat and cold. "This... this man is the one responsible for...?" He couldn't bring himself to say it.

"All the evidence points to him. We are still trying to determine if he acted alone or with others. He is a werewolf, but it was also not a full moon. I've never heard of anything like it before. But then again a lot has changed in five years."

"Yes, yes it has," Lucas murmurs, his frown deepening. "He seems so... normal."

"All of them do," Tim says with a heavy sigh. "All monsters appear normal. Human or not."

~*~

It was all too much to take and for a few moments she just let herself cry into the pillow, letting it all out. The pain was sharp and raw, worse than anything that beast had physically done to her. Lucas had set her up. He hand-picked the werewolf to murder her, to rip her out of the equation completely, so he could...

The thought was left unfinished to a fresh bout of sobs, and for a long time she just lay there, her heart broken and feeling helpless to do anything about it. A divorce would have been easy, even if it had been dragged out into the open by the media and milked dry by salivating lawyers. Now he could soak up the benefits of being a widower and a single parent and his stocks would soar. Her poor son would grow up without his mother and never know his father was the one who plotted her vicious and public murder. What was worse, the world might never have known if she had been torn apart in that alley, if Korban hadn't been there to rescue her from the beast's jaws.

Staring at the wall with blurry eyes, she tried to figure her next step. The fact was she had survived. The world could know about what happened to her, if she was brave enough to step out into the spotlight and expose Lucas for what he did. Her fear remained, not of endangering herself, but of putting Daniel in the next set of crosshairs. She had to get him to safety first, if only there was someone she could trust-

Nikki. It came to her suddenly, and despite her earlier reservations of letting anyone know she was still alive, her son's safety outweighed her own. She had to let her sister know, and had to get her son away from Lucas before she exposed him.

Before she could talk herself out of it, she spotted a cell phone laying on the dresser and scooped it up, dialing the one number she'd memorized by heart. The phone rang three times, and then the familiar but puzzled voice answered, "Who's this?"

"Nikki, it's Sophie," she blurted, her heart swelling in relief as fresh tears rushed down her cheeks. "I'm sorry I didn't call sooner, I know you all must be so worried, but please, before you say anything, you have to trust me and not say anything to anyone around you right now-"

Through the phone she could hear her sister's breath catch, then the clicking of heels as she quickly moved, the creak of a door hinge, and then the snap of a lock. "*Sophie?*" Nikki whispered in disbelief. "You're alive?! Oh thank God! When that monster took you away like that, I completely lost it! Where are you? Are you still hurt? Should I call the police, or an ambulance, or-"

"Nikki, please," she interrupted to plead, "you can't tell anyone right now. I can't explain it this moment, but you have to trust me. You and Danny could both be in a lot of danger right now. I need you to take him to Mom and Dad's as soon as possible."

"What's going on, Sophie? You were attacked and we all thought you were dead and now- where are you? I need to see you! I want to see you!" Nikki pleaded, still whispering, the anxiety pouring through the phone.

"I'm fine, please Nikki, you have to believe me. Just tell Lucas you want to take Danny up to get him away from the media circus that is surrounding right now. Take him to Mom and Dad's, and stay there too. Please do this for me," Sophie begged. "I want to know you are both safe."

Nikki only breathed on the other end for a long moment, then whimpered again, "I just want to see you. I was so scared that I'd never see you again, that- that thing ate you and-" She sniffled, "please Sissy, where are you? I want to help you but I want to see you with my own eyes! The last time I saw you that monster was tearing you apart!"

As much as she wanted to see her sister in that moment, she had to stay strong. "Not now, Nikki, but I promise you soon I can see you. Just please take Danny to Florida. It's the best place for you both to be right now. Make it look like it was Lucas' idea and get out of Syracuse. I'm safe here, I'm with good friends and they are helping me lay low. I promise I'll call in a few days and explain everything, okay?"

Nikki sobbed then sniffled loudly again. "Okay. Give me a couple days and I can get Danny out of here, but you better call me- this number you're calling from is unlisted, are you sure you can't give me it?"

"No, Nikki, I'm sorry. No one can know where I'm at right now. I don't want to put you in any danger if I can help it." Sophie trembled, wiping the tears from her eyes. "I'll call you in three days, I swear it, and when I do I'll explain everything. I have to go, please keep Danny and yourself safe in the meantime. And whatever you do, don't let Lucas talk you out of going."

"Okay, Sissy."

Before Nikki could talk her into anything else, she said her goodbyes and hung up the phone. She cleared the call from the call list and set it back down on the dresser. She laid down on the bed, feeling much more relieved now that at least Nikki and Danny would soon be safely away from any of Lucas' diabolical schemes.

~*~

The press release would be handled by his office goddess Patty, who even offered to call him a cab home which Tim declined graciously. As exhausted as he was the ride home helped him unwind. And today he was in desperate need of that lonely road. He starts the engine of his ancient F10, rubs his weary eyes and cranks up the volume on the Lynyrd Skynyrd on the radio. He rolls the window down and as he turns onto the highway the rush of chilly spring air invigorates him. The guitar riffs rip away the long hours, the drums pound away the gory scenes he witnessed. The burden of work lifts from his shoulders with every mile he puts behind him, the rusty but reliable truck chugging towards the familiar release that was home.

It was during these precious stress-relieving moments that his exhausted mind was recharging, able to finally process all the information of the day. The combination of fresh air and the adrenaline of speeding on the highway to some classic rock seemed to finally fire the weary synapses in his brain.

Brett Kensington was the one who crashed the gala and

murdered Sophie Bane. Of this much he was sure. They would have to wait a few days to find out the source of all the blood at the cabin, but without anyone able to get a hold of the man's family it seemed their fate remained as grim as the crime scene. He wondered back at the station how any man could just throw their whole life away for some twisted fan boy dream. Who would do such a thing? Who would risk their family's lives for fleeting, uncontrollable strength?

Who?

Who, indeed. It dawned on him very suddenly, he pumps the breaks as the thought bubbles to the surface.

They, Brett had confessed. *They* had given him a serum. It had caused him to black out, wake in the dumpster after the deed had been done. But who were "they"?

Who had given Kensington the serum?

And who had infected the man to begin with?

He'd been asking the wrong questions, trying to ease the mind of a wealthy widower. This case on the surface appeared closed, but there were so many unresolved questions. Someone helped Kensington become a werewolf, giving him the reassurance that he would be fine with some mystery medication that may have cost Sophie Bane and Kensington's own family their lives. There was more to this, he knew it in his gut.

Tim pulls over to the side of the highway, ignoring the horns that blared at him in protest. He yanks out his cell phone and dials his partner's number. Andy answers, his voice groggy and he almost feels sorry that he'd waken him up. "This better be good, McKinnon."

"Someone else is involved in all this," Tim blurts, wasting no time on formalities. "Someone is setting up Kensington."

"Setting up a werewolf to eat a rich man's wife and his own family? Who would do that, and how would that even be possible?"

"He mentioned 'they' and a serum. Whatever it was he took must have forced the change. Mrs. Bane wasn't attacked during a full moon." Unlike the Kensington family, he thought grimly.

"Okay, and you're right, someone had to infect him. Something made him a werewolf." He can hear the tinny sound of old springs and knew Andy was still at the station, he'd probably passed out in the old armchair in the break room. "Kensington… we were looking into him before all this, following up with your monthly check in with Korban Diego, right? He mentioned how Kensington was looking for a biter and willing to pay big. Maybe he found someone. I can log in and check his bank records. Everything was seized once we brought him into custody."

"Good thinking Ellyk. See what turns up." The exit for home was tantalizingly close, he could see it ahead in the distance. He couldn't give in to the siren's song, not when they were this close to a new break in the case.

He could hear Andy cussing under his breath as he clicked away at the keyboard. The turning signal drummed a note slower than his heartbeat. "Sonovabitch," Andy swears after a long moment. "No payments out, but it looks like a pretty large amount of cash was deposited into his account two weeks ago. I don't know of many people in this city who would have that much cash to take out, McKinnon… unless…" He trails off, but Tim can easily finish the thought. Lucas Bane was one of the few who would have that much laying around.

Something told him they had just begun to scratch the surface on this investigation. They'd need a warrant to search Bane's financial records to see if there was a matching amount missing from his account, but even if they were to get a warrant the banks wouldn't be open until tomorrow morning. He tries to think of anyone who owed him that huge of a favor, but the hour is stretching his overworked brain thin. "We can try and interrogate it out of Kensington first thing tomorrow while we get Patty on digging up connections to the bank. Either way we both need to recharge and there isn't much we can do until the banks open up tomorrow."

"Sleep. Now that is an idea I can get on board with," Andy agrees, and Tim can hear the springs settle again loudly as his partner sinks back on the ancient armchair. "Go home Tim. Get some shut eye and don't call me again until the sun is over the dome, got it? Even Bruce Wayne has to sleep."

His brilliant brainstorm and the rush from it was starting to fade, and he was suddenly very thankful that his exit was right there. "Wayne Manor, here I come. G'night, Ellyk."

"See you tomorrow McKinnon."

~*~

She attempted to sleep, but when Sophie closed her eyes those glowing amber eyes stared at her from behind her eyelids. If it wasn't the beast it was Lucas, so many lies hidden behind his charming smile. Worse yet were the brief night terrors the images twisted into when exhaustion finally consumed her. Watching her husband fade off with her son and some mystery woman in tow, who shifted into a leering wolf and bayed to the red moon above them all.

Suddenly she was awake, trembling and sitting straight up. Her mouth was as dry as cotton. She glanced to the alarm clock, and the dimly glowing digits revealed 4:31 am. Only a meager two hours of sleep.

She got up and wrapped Korban's robe around herself. She wasn't really cold but felt chilled inside, and something about the warm robe with his scent all over it soothed her. Sophie quietly opened the bedroom door, padding quietly out into the hall.

Alex and RJ's light snoring let her know that they were sleeping blissfully up the hall. To her surprise, when she entered the living room Korban wasn't there. The door to the roof was slightly ajar, the cool night air trickling in.

When she walked out onto the rooftop, Korban was sitting alone on the far edge, staring out at the sliver of moon. As she approached he turned, managing a smile, though it wasn't as brilliant as usual. "Hey," he said softly.

"Hey," she smiled in turn to him, though it was strained as well. She knew now something wasn't right.

She sat down beside him and gazed out into the night. It was amazing to see the city at night, some windows glowing as bright as the stars even this late. The view wasn't what brought Korban out here, though, and so she reached to him as he reached to her before. Touching his arm, she asked gently, "If it helps, you can talk to me."

He offered her another small smile, "My problems aren't as bad compared to what you're going through right now, I think."

She stared at him for a moment, then said, "That doesn't mean you have to hold them in, or that they aren't as important."

He exhaled with a sigh, focusing on something unseen in the distance. At first, it seemed he wouldn't talk. Then he turned to her, a pained expression in his eyes, "The night I was turned I lost my best friend."

Her gaze softens in sympathy. He had mentioned this before, but it was obvious that this was difficult for him to discuss. She could be patient and listen. He'd already done so much more for her.

"We were more than best friends and closer than brothers. Both of us were raised by our mothers, and didn't have our fathers in our lives. Birds of a feather, my mom used to say. Mom even took Ace in after his mother went missing.

"We were coming home after a party. Alex drank too much so RJ told us to go ahead, he'd catch up with us later. Since RJ could handle him on his own, we didn't think too much about it. We knew the streets, even drunk. Especially drunk.

"I thought it was just some huge stray dog. Some of those suckers get pretty big, and vicious. But when I looked into its eyes it sobered me right up. I knew it was hunting me. I knew that it was going to kill me." He trembled and she put a gentle hand on his arm. She'd thought her attack had been brutal enough, not seeing the beast coming. Apparently the alternative was no better.

"All I can remember is... were those eyes. Glowing, yellow. They might as well have been red," he paused for a long moment, then released a breath he hadn't realized he'd been holding. "When I woke up, there was this noise... a terrible sound, like a high-pitched scream that wouldn't stop. It made my head hurt so bad I thought my skull was splitting open. It was my first time hearing police and ambulance sirens with the wolf's ears." He gave a small smirk, then gazed back to the city. "Ace, my best friend. They put him on the stretcher. He was so still, so pale. They wouldn't let me go near him. They tied me down on the stretcher and I was too weak to break free. Even with the wolf inside me."

Her hand moved again, resting on top of his. He returned his gaze up to hers, golden eyes locking with her emerald ones. She tried to picture him with brown eyes, but it didn't stick in her mind. The gold suited him.

They were so close together at that moment... she could smell him, under the faint aftershave and mouthwash. His scent was safe, familiar; and yet wild and alluring. She heard his heartbeat speed up, and wanted to close that gap between them. Leaning in, she heard his breath catch, and then-

The echo of sirens in the distance. Police searching for her. Maybe Nikki and Danny-

She offered a shaky smile as she pulled away. Her hand remained rested on his. While she could resist a kiss, she couldn't stand to pull her hand from his. Not just yet.

12: MASSACRE

Korban didn't sleep much that night, unable to get rid of the rush of adrenaline that came from Sophie holding his hand. She had stayed there with him for a long time, then quietly said good night and returned to bed. He moved from the roof to the living room, paced in the garage for awhile, then finally ended up sitting at the kitchen table with yesterday's *Post Standard* spread in front of him, staring at the front page but not even reading the headline. All he could see was her, his hand still warm from her skin and her scent lingering on his.

RJ blinked when he emerged from his own bedroom, raising an eyebrow. "You're up early today," he commented, then rubbed his eyes. "You could have put the coffee on, that might have been nice."

"Oh right. I'm sorry," Korban couldn't hide a goofy grin that made RJ stare at him, even as he got up and pulled the coffee tin from the cupboard.

He caught a glimpse of RJ's amused smile as he began to measure out the coffee, the strong, wonderful scent nothing compared to hers. "Did I miss something last night? You're in a pretty good mood."

Korban attempted to busy himself with the coffee, putting a lot more effort into it than necessary to hide the blush that was surely creeping across his face. "Nothing, it's nothing." As the coffee began to percolate he moved to gathering the mugs, cream and sugar. "You want your usual half and half, or would you rather have milk today?"

RJ folded his arms over his chest and smirked. "Changing the subject doesn't work well on teachers, Korban. I thought you of all people would know that."

There was no hiding anything from RJ. Korban set the carton of cream on the counter. "Sophie came up on the roof last night and we talked."

"Talked?" RJ repeated, scratching his chin. "You're acting like the two of you did a hell of a lot more than just talking up there. You didn't, did you?"

Korban blinked at him, then quickly shook his head, "No, it wasn't like that. Sophie has other things on her mind right now, which is definitely understandable." He glanced to the coffee pot, which was steadily filling with every drip. "She held my hand."

RJ seemed to struggle a moment, then his lips formed a small smile, "You're going gaga because she held your hand, Korban? I never realized you were the romantic type."

"I know, it's stupid, but-"

RJ shook his head. "It's not stupid, Korban. Feelings are never stupid. We can't help what we feel. She's been through a lot, and you've been there for her in this really difficult time." He paused. "I just hope that you don't end up hurt. You've been through a lot too, Korban."

"Yeah," Korban said softly, rubbing his temples as he leaned over the counter. "I care about her, and I want her to be happy.

Seeing how far she's come already, it makes me so proud. You remember what it was like. It was months before I was able to be in a room with another human being."

"That may be true, but what they did to you was wrong. Taking you away from people who gave a damn and throwing you into some sick observation facility, especially after you watched Ace-" RJ's voice caught when he saw Korban tense, and he moved on from his point. "It's no wonder you couldn't stand to have another person around you. You were hurting, and if it wasn't for some lucky reporter getting the scoop that night we might have never known what happened to you. You could have been a missing person, or worse if they were really trying to cover up your disappearance."

Korban nodded grimly at that, staring at the dark liquid filling the coffee pot. "I don't want anyone else to suffer like that, especially Sophie. Even if we expose Lucas for what he did to her, what will happen next? Will they take her away to one of those places after they arrest Lucas? She has a son, RJ. He's under the age restriction, she won't be allowed near him at all. Her own son. What will happen to him? "

RJ gave a heavy sigh, "I wish I had the answers, but until Lucas is behind bars for what he did you know Sophie isn't safe."

The folder was still laying on the table where they left it, and Korban's gaze was drawn in that direction. "I can't believe someone would do something like this to the woman they married, someone they supposedly love. What kind of sick person would do such a thing?"

"I don't know why he would set up Sophie to die in such a violent attack. It's not for us to understand. What is important now is that you are here to help Sophie, just like we were there for you. You saved her life and you are helping her get her feet back on the ground. None of this makes any sense, but when did anything we ever did before make sense anyway?" He smiled to his friend, clapping a hand on his shoulder. "There will be a hell of a lot of backlash from exposing Lucas Bane with that file. Maybe you should take the time to enjoy the calm before the storm."

Seeing that mischievous glint return in RJ's eyes, a slow smile crept across Korban's face, "Thanks, RJ."

"What are friends for?" he said, nodding to the coffee which had just finished. "Nothing like good conversation and a cup of Joe to start the day." He playfully punched Korban's shoulder, "Let's get a cup and check out the headlines. I have a feeling we'll be stopping the presses with news of our own tonight."

~*~

The calm as RJ put it did not last long, and the news hit like a hurricane with that morning's paper - expected and yet even worse than imaginable. Korban stared at the newspaper and wasn't sure how to digest today's headline. All he could think about was how he was going to break the news to Sophie.

Sophie, whose smiling photo was splashed on the front page, under the morbidly eye-catching headline, "WOLVEN MASSACRE". Next to her picture was a smiling family in front of a cabin, a plain but pretty brunette woman and two children- a boy with scruffy brown hair and a grin missing a few teeth, and a little girl who beamed from the arms of her father, a man with a familiar face, though it wasn't until he read the byline that it clicked into his memory- Brett Kensington, the man who wanted to become a werewolf. A man that tragically got his wish and now had destroyed the lives of so many- including his own wife and children, and Sophie.

The pieces snapped into place, the name scrawled on the paper in the file they found at the Bane condo. Brett Kensington had found someone crazy enough to follow through with his plan after all. Korban didn't realize he was growling until the sound suddenly snapped him out of his own thoughts. He wanted to shred this newspaper to ribbons and howl out his frustration and rage. Kensington hadn't heeded his warning. Now Sophie was suffering the consequences and those poor kids and Mrs. Kensington... and yet, as foolish as the man had been it was the one who enabled him that set all this in motion.

"Um... so now might be a bad time to bring up the whole leaving dishes in the sink without rinsing them thing," Alex's voice cracked nervously, causing Korban to glance his way. He hadn't even heard his roommate enter the room, but clearly from the look on his face he'd been there for his growl. "Uh... you aren't gonna attack too, right? I just washed these pants."

"No, unless your name is Lucas Bane you're safe from me," Korban growls out, tossing the newspaper onto the kitchen table. He began to pace around the room. "I told him not to go through with it. I'd hoped to talk sense into him. If I'd only gotten through, maybe those kids would still be around. Maybe Sophie would still have a normal life. Maybe if-"

"Whoa, whoa, Korban. Dude," Alex approaches him catching him by the arms and for a brief moment there is fear in the mechanic's eyes when their eyes meet, but his resolve breaks through. "Do. Not. Blame. Yourself." He emphasizes each word and keeps his brown eyes trained on him. "What happened to all of them... you can't blame yourself. You did everything you could. The ifs and maybes won't do you any good. What's done is done. No one can change the past. We can only go forward from here."

He was right and Korban knew it, but he hated the fact that everything that happened seemed to lead back to him. No, Alex was right. It lead back to the one who enabled this cruel plan from the beginning. Korban felt guilty for his failed warnings, but the failure wasn't on him. Someone was sick enough to allow Kensington's warped wish to come true. And the cost hadn't mattered. Kensington's family and Sophie were the ones who paid the price but they hadn't mattered to the one behind this tragedy.

A sickening feeling twisted in his gut. Kensington had been used as a weapon and he would be the one taking the fall. He may have been the teeth and claws but there was another hand in this. "Someone set up the perfect crime. They didn't plan on Sophie surviving. They wanted Kensington to take the fall for this, so it looked like the blood wasn't on their hands." Korban picks up the folder on the table and opens it, looking at the list scrawled on the paper again. The name on the sheet- B. Kensington- and the other times and notes. "How could such a well devised plan neglect to remove all the evidence?"

"You said it," Alex says, letting his gaze roam the newspaper with a sigh. "They hadn't planned on Sophie returning home. The file was unmarked. He never imagined she would be back to see it, and he never expected you'd be there to help her through this. If anything, Korban, you saved Sophie's life."

It did make him feel better, though his stomach still clenched with guilt when he saw the family photo on the front page. His eyes move to the picture of Sophie and he sighs. "How... how do I even begin to explain this to Sophie?"

"She's an intelligent lady, I think she'll understand," Alex says, but Korban shakes his head.

"I know that, it's not a question about her intelligence, it's just... she's already been through so much and... her husband may be behind all this, and now-"

"Now... what?" Sophie's voice came as she peered at the pair of them from the hallway.

Korban can smell the anxiety in Alex peak slightly, as well as in Sophie- but it passes quickly. She approached slowly and Alex timidly steps behind Korban- though she smiles a little at him. "I think I'm getting used to you. I promise I'm not going to tackle you today."

"Well there goes this morning's plans," Alex jokes back with a smile. "I suppose I'll just have to get to work and be productive instead."

She smiles to him again, relaxing a little more. Her eyes meet Korban's and he knows as difficult as it was he couldn't lie to her. She deserved the truth as much as he wanted to protect her from it. The truth would only come out and he wouldn't be the one to hold back on her. Especially after how deceiving her husband had been. "Now I think we have another piece to the puzzle, though it's not a pretty one," Korban hands her the newspaper and Sophie accepts it, reading over the headline and frowning at the pictures.

"So this is the man who attacked me... he seems so... normal." Her bright blue eyes go round when she sees she wasn't his only victim. "Those poor kids... his wife..."

"I tried to warn him. I told him that the state would keep him in quarantine, that he'd never get to see them again." The guilt, despite himself, still churned inside of Korban. "He didn't listen."

"You knew him?" Sophie blinks in surprise and he quickly nods.

"Not personally but... remember the night we first met? He's the one who brought me in for a job interview only to ask me to turn him instead."

"He..." Sophie's gaze turns solemn as she looks back at the paper. "He actually *chose* to do this?"

Korban nods again, at a loss for words as an array of emotions flicker across Sophie's face. Shock. Anger. Grief. Everything he'd felt at the news himself.

"You turned him down, you wouldn't bite him," Sophie says as a sudden calm courses through her, then the rage rears its head in her. "So he found someone else who said yes. This man's name was on that list. Lucas... he has the resources. He could have gotten a willing werewolf and... and..." It was Sophie's turn to growl, and this time Alex takes that as his sign to leave and ducks out to the garage. "That stupid man lost his family and nearly killed me! It's a good thing that bastard is behind bars or I'd throttle him myself! How could he be that selfish? How could he just throw it all away- his family- just to... to..." Something in the article catches her eye and she trails off, her hands shaking and the sound of crinkling paper fills the air. "My... memorial service... is today?!" She blinks in disbelief, and the paper starts to rip a little in her trembling, tense hands. "They... they really do believe I'm dead. Lucas thinks he got away with murder."

"He thinks so, but we know the truth," Korban goes to her, putting a comforting hand on her shoulder. Her entire body was shaking.

The newspaper suddenly flops to the floor and Sophie whirls around, facing Korban with an intense look in her eyes. Fierce determination was there. "He won't get away with this. I won't let him." Her eyes move back to the file they'd uncovered. "We need to get this information to the police. Even if it means revealing that I'm alive. I can't let this go down like this. That man may have attacked me but he was set up. His family paid the ultimate price and... and that's bad enough. We need to go to them with what we know, Korban."

He knew she was right. They had to do the right thing, even if it put a target on Sophie again. She couldn't hide forever. His worry was clearly something she could sense and she suddenly takes his hand in hers. "I know you want to protect me, Korban. But we cannot allow him to get away with this."

Her touch as always sends a rush through him. Yes, he did want to protect her. The knot in his stomach loosens a little at the look in her eyes. She had resolved to do this, and it was that strength and spirit that had made his initial attraction to her grow into the love he felt now. "You're right," he says. "I'll give Tim a call. If the news is gonna break… we may as well let him know first."

Sophie nods, and gives Korban's hand a tender squeeze. "Thank you again, for all of this. I know you are risking so much for me. You, RJ, and Alex."

"That's what friends are for, right?" Korban smiles a little, but that is when her hand catches him by the collar and tugs him close.

Her blue eyes were suddenly closer, vibrant as the winter sky, the tiniest flecks of the wolf's amber glistening amidst the sapphire hues. For the briefest moment confusion sets in, and then her lips meet his, so soft and warm, and welcoming. Her hand slides up his collar, behind his neck, and her fingertips lightly rake through his short hair. He is vaguely aware of her other hand as it glides up his chest, over his pounding heart, to move up and meet the other hand behind his neck.

His arms wrap around her as she guides his mouth to part for her and their kiss deepens. His senses are completely consumed by her, his mouth dancing with hers, his tongue indulging in her sweet taste. He's dizzy when she finally pulls away, though her arms remain around him, his hands resting at the small of her back. Surely if his heart continued to race like this it would burst.

A smile curves her lips and with the taste of them still on his own Korban wanted nothing more than to capture them again, and again. It dawns on him then how that had been his first kiss since he'd been bitten and how amazing it was- the rush that was going through him only intensified. And with the look she gave him clearly he wasn't the only one who felt the high from their brief interlude.

Her hands remain at the nape of his neck, fingertips lightly combing through his hair, sending delightful shivers through his scalp, down through his body. "You've done more for me than anyone else has, Korban, and asked for nothing in return. You've proven that you are far more than just a friend. When... when all this is over... I want you to know just how much you mean to me too. No matter what happens."

His heart skips a beat, swelling with so much emotion. "Sophie, I..."

"Shh," she cuts him off with another kiss, and another few moments they are lost in mutual bliss, until she reluctantly pulls away. "We... we can figure this out later. First we need to make sure justice is served."

Korban nods, feeling rather flustered and breathless. He's still a little stunned and it takes him a moment to collect himself. Remembering what he was about to do, he picks up the phone and dials Tim's number from memory. It rings several times then his voicemail picks up.

"This is Sergeant Tim McKinnon with the Syracuse Police Department, I may be on the other line or out of the office, but if you leave your name, phone number, and a message I'll get back at ya as soon as possible. Thanks and make it a great day."

The tell-tale beep sounded and Korban, still a bit flustered, cleared his throat and began, "Hey Tim, it's me, Korban. I uh... I need to talk to you about something but I think it would be better in person. Give me a call when you can. Thanks." He hangs up the phone and looks to Sophie. "He must be busy but he'll call back. I... I hope you don't mind. I just- I feel much better revealing all this to him first. Someone who we can trust, and also... I don't want any backlash to come from this, particularly for RJ. He loves teaching those kids and he doesn't need this coming back to him."

Sophie gives him a small, slightly guilty smile. "I don't want any of you guys getting in trouble over this. You have all been more than kind and understanding. Lucas will be served his justice. If it means waiting a little longer to make sure you guys will be okay I don't mind the anticipation. He will get what's coming to him."

13: WOLVEN

At the rate this was going, Tim was sure that he would need to pop something much stronger than aspirin to keep his growing migraine at bay. The Kensington case was now the hottest news of the day, with the sensational headlines and the public intrigue over the very public assault on Sophie Bane and the tragic murders of the picturesque Kensington family. What hadn't been released to the public was the information Andy had unearthed, a large cash deposit in Kensington's bank account. Patty was still making calls and they had no solid evidence to issue another warrant on Kensington's mysterious benefactor. Which is why after barely four and a half hours of sleep both Ellyk and himself were once again in an interrogation room with Brett Kensington sitting across from them, clearly miserable and in silver handcuffs. "You are really trying our patience here, tough guy," Andy glares coldly at the mousy man-werewolf. "Even cash is traceable. You'll be saving a lot of work hours and headaches if you would just tell us who paid you, Kensington. Who is the source of your lycanthropy? Who set you up to kill Sophie Bane? Who enabled you to destroy your family? Your kids?" He shoves the newspaper across the table, and Kensington's eyes fix on the image there- his pale mug shot, Sophie Bane smiling, his wife and kids smiling alongside him in front of the cabin where they would meet their grisly demise.

Playing good cop, Tim folds his arms over his chest. "It doesn't look good, but again, you play nice and maybe we can arrange a deal so the review board will go easy on you."

Kensington stares wordlessly at the front page. Dark circles under his eyes showed that he hadn't slept much either. If anything he was even thinner and paler than the mug shot now. Maybe he finally snapped. "What does it matter. It's done and I am doomed," he says in a hollow tone. "They're gone... and even if I told you it wouldn't bring them back. I can only stall the inevitable. I can suffer longer for this if I say nothing. Once you have all the pieces I'm expendable."

Damn it, Kensington was no fool, even if he had made foolish choices leading him to this moment. "Look, we can do this dance some more but the truth is you're right. There's no fucking way you'll see the light of day once we close this case," Tim cut to the chase, "but I can tell you this: whoever it was who hooked you up with the money and the lycanthropy virus, they set you up big time. You want them to get away with using you like a weapon? With the murders of your kids, wife, and Mrs. Bane?"

Kensington stares up at him with that haunted, empty look. A tiny spark seemed to ignite in him at the words as they sunk in.

"You're their fall guy, don't you get it? They royally screwed you over. Sure, they gave you what you wanted. You wanted to be a werewolf so bad and they exploited that, to make sure their ends met. And remind me, Kensington... where's your benefactor now? Now that you're stuck behind bars and your family and the Bane family have buried those they lost? Was this part of their plan, or are you really involved in this on a whole other level? Because let me tell you, my years on this force I've seen some pretty messed up shit, but never something this selfishly short-sighted and severely despicable. If you had a hand- or claw- in not only murdering but devouring your own family and-"

"ENOUGH!" Kensington snarls suddenly, standing and smacking his hands on the table, despite the silver restraints, and leaving sizable dents in the metal table. "I've heard enough of your accusations! I wanted to become a werewolf, yes. I had no intention of ever hurting anyone! Especially my kids," His voice cracks with emotion. "I just wanted to be stronger. To be a hero in their eyes. To be a real man for them, for my wife. They told me I could control it, if I used the serum I could handle the change and be in control. But it only made things worse. I black out, and then Sophie Bane is dead. I call them up and suddenly there's nothing, no word back. I figure I lay low, take the family and get out of dodge. Then... the full moon... God, why didn't I even look at the calendar?" He runs his hands through his hair, the silver cuffs clanking, his wrists raw and burning from the jostling of the precious metal. "It is my fault. All my fault. I should have listened to the other werewolf. I should have..." He trails off again, his breathing becoming labored.

"Kensington?" Andy asks, his frown deepening.

"You have no idea what it's like," Brett's voice is soft, filled with pain. "Waking up, thinking you escaped a nightmare. Only to find out that the dream is over, that what you wake up to is even worse. That the nightmare has really only just begun."

Tim almost felt sorry for the broken man, but this had been the man's own doing. He may have not set out to murder Sophie Bane or his family, but his selfish actions had destroyed lives. Kensington sags down again looking lost. "If you tell us who hooked you up... sure, it may not put you in a better position. But what about the spirits of your two kids, your wife, Mrs. Bane? Don't they at least deserve peace after their violent and sudden end?"

Brett only chuckles mirthlessly. "You telling me now officer that there are ghosts in the world?"

Tim frowns. "I'm tellin' you that the only way you'll be finding that one out is if you keep playing around. If you even want a remote chance to return to quarantine instead of biting a silver bullet, you'd better reconsider cooperating with us. We're your last chance of redemption."

Kensington leans back and gives another cold chuckle. "No one can redeem me. I'm way beyond damned now."

A knock comes and the door opens without further warning. A young sandy-haired, familiar officer peers in. With all hands on deck for this case, even the greenest of rookies were assigned to help out and Tim only knew the kid by his badge, branding him as Parker. "Uh, sorry to interrupt, Sergeant. The Commissioner's getting antsy and the press are swarming the station. She wants to have Kensington relocated to Hutchings sooner rather than later, before it gets worse out there."

Well. It wasn't divine intervention exactly, but someone was looking over Kensington. Andy frowned and Tim scratched the goatee on his chin. "She wants to move him now?"

"Her orders," the rookie shrugs. "I don't question them, I'm not anywhere close to having tenure. She says that you can continue your interrogation there, in a more secure facility."

Andy grunts. "All right. Let's get this mongrel to his new cage then. Maybe he'll be singing a different tune when he sees just what kind of hospitality awaits him."

Hutchings was a well-known psychiatric hospital that now also served as a facility for those infected from the outbreak. Newly infected persons were sent there in quarantine and closely monitored and observed before given their clearance and assigned to a trustworthy citizen- their handler- and reintegrated back into society. The past five years only about one in every ten infected were cleared to rejoin the world at large, and the paper work was horrendous.

People like Korban were lucky to get their freedom back at all, even if it came with lengthy and strictly enforced rules of behavior. The rooms at Hutchings would definitely be more secure than their jail, but even Kensington had to grasp the fact that many went into quarantine and only a select few were released.

"Looks like our party will have to continue there," Tim nods to Andy who picks up a metal mask device that was reminiscent to the one worn by Hannibal Lecter and puts the muzzle back on the man, who doesn't even fight him, just continues to stare down at the printed images of his victims and the headline.

~*~

"This is Sergeant Tim McKinnon with-" Even across the room, Sophie can hear the familiar recorded message play over again. Korban clicks off the phone and frowns, worry creasing his brow. "Now it's going straight to voicemail," he sighed, scratching the back of his head. "That's really strange. Tim never turns off his phone."

Three hours had passed, the morning gone and moving into a rather comfortable afternoon. Sunlight streamed in, warming her skin. Korban glanced to his phone as if trying to will Tim's return call with a look, but to no avail. She could sense the anxiety coming from him, the scent of the strong emotion in the air. Not that she needed to be able to smell it to realize he was tense- it sang through his body, muscles tight and twitching. Watching him pace was exhausting, and she sat down on the comfortable, worn couch. "Still no luck then," Sophie frowns, leaning back and crossing her legs on the sofa.

"No, unfortunately," Korban sighs, setting the phone down on the coffee table. "He has busy days, but usually by now he'd call back. I can't get through to the station either."

She picks up the remote control and points it at the television. "Maybe something big has happened."

The screen clicks to life and the image that appears is something straight out of *The Twilight Zone*. Sophie had been through some very strange things, especially as of late, but this was way too surreal. The local stations were all covering it, and each channel that she flipped to captured the macabre scene. She wanted to turn away but Sophie sat, feeling numb yet mesmerized by the events unfolding before her on the television screen.

Lucas, looking solemn and not dazzling the camera with his usual smile and suaveness. In fact, in the camera lights it was clear that he had dark circles under his eyes. Next to him little Daniel stood, holding his father's hand and looking so miserable that it broke her heart. In his hand that wasn't clutching onto his father's was a single red rose.

Her heart ached, and though part of her wanted desperately to look away, the sight of her son alive and whole but utterly devastated… A lump formed in her throat, and as much as it pained her she couldn't turn away.

The casket was a polished white box, elegant and covered with a lush bouquet of colorful flowers. She spotted her sister alongside Lucas and Daniel, wearing a stylish but conservative black dress. Nikki was red-faced and dabbing her eyes with a handkerchief. Her parents were huddled together next to Nikki, her father looking crushed and even more upset than her mother. Of course, her mother had always been the stronger of the pair.

The newscasters would pan the cameras over the gathered family; aunts, uncles and cousins she hadn't seen in years. Faces familiar and strange blended in together in black suits and dresses. Every once in a while they would show the elegantly arranged coffin and a smiling portrait of her. Sophie remembered the day that photo had been taken. It seemed like that was a stranger smiling back now, with vivid blue eyes and a carefree smile.

It was eerie to watch her own funeral. It was heartbreakingly horrific to watch her family mourn her. Yet like a cliché train wreck, as terrible was it was she couldn't look away. Her eyes remained glued to the screen. She felt both agonized and strangely unattached, like if she turned away it wouldn't be her funeral but someone else's. More than anything she stared at her young son. Her grief for him was more powerful than even her own turmoil. She wished she could wrap her arms around him and make things right with words and butterfly kisses.

She wondered if she would ever get the chance to hold her son again. Pain shot through her heart at the mere thought of never… she felt tears well up in her eyes, the images on the television suddenly blurred to the point of an impressionist painting. She was so raw with hurt that she didn't even hear or smell Korban until he was suddenly there, a comforting arm draped around her. She tensed at first, her wolf and human sides equally startled. When she inhaled the scent of forest and fur that came from him the tension melted away. As strong as she was this was too much.

Danny crying, believing she was dead and gone. Her entire family clad in black and mourning her. All because all they found were the scraps of her dress, drenched in her blood. The words of some poor bastard who believed he had murdered and devoured her…

She sagged against Korban and let out a long exhale, not even aware that she had been holding her breath. Warm, wet tears began to fall and she didn't have the strength to stop them. Korban wisely said nothing, or perhaps he was simply at a loss for words. She didn't trust her own voice at the moment. She was sure that if she opened her mouth she would release an anguished howl that she wouldn't be able to stop.

Korban gazed from the scene to her, then back again. He opened his mouth, but then closed it again. He looked at her worriedly.

"I…" Sophie croaked after a long moment. "I don't know if I can do this. All I want to do is go and run to him. To let Danny know that I'm okay."

Korban nodded, and though he didn't know the extent of her pain personally he could sympathize. The look in his eyes seemed to mirror her own pain.

"I… I am too dangerous to be around him. I know that. But to see him like this… at my funeral… all I want to do is run to him." Sophie wrung her hands together and they were shaking. She turns away from the television as it pans again over the gathered crowd of mourners and looks into Korban's golden eyes. "I want Lucas to pay for this. I want justice. But right now… I need out. I need to go. I just need to breathe…" She needed a distraction of cosmic proportions but maybe just a few hours out, away from this torment that held her within these four walls.

Something flashes in Korban's eyes and he nods. "Let's go then."

She blinks to him, wiping the corners of her eyes delicately with the back of her knuckles. She wasn't sure how he was going to respond and asks, "Where? Where can we go now?"

"Anywhere we want to," Korban says, taking her trembling hands into his and giving hers a tender squeeze. "One of the only plus sides of all of Central New York believing you're gone is no one will be looking for you now. We can go anywhere you like."

Anywhere but where he was, she knew, but before she could linger on the thought she blurts out, "Show me where you go to get away and just breathe. I want to see your side of town. I want to see where you grew up, where you go to escape. It can't always be on the roof."

Korban gives her a small smile and nods, "All right."

~*~

They accompany Kensington as they guide him towards the rear exit, where the rookie guided them to where a van transport was waiting. Tim could already hear the murmurs of the crowd waiting outside, swarming the area with cameras, microphones, lights, and cell phones. Which reminded him. He glanced at his own phone, seeing several missed calls and voicemail messages from Korban Diego. He'd have to call him after they transported Kensington to the facility at Hutchings. Slipping his cell phone back into his pocket he continues to guide the werewolf with Ellyk through the doors and into the awaiting chaos.

Cameras and heads turned, all eyes on them. Tim feels Kensington tense and a frightened whine emerges from the werewolf. Even as a predator the man was a coward. They guide their quarry towards the van despite the barrage of questions, camera lights flashing, shouted comments, and even a few screams.

"Mr. Kensington! Care to comment?"

"Is it true you devoured Sophie Bane?"

"Did you assault Mrs. Bane to cover up your illicit affair?"

Tim tried not to roll his eyes and urged Kensington along with Andy. The doors to the van are open when the sound of something whizzed past and there is a sharp ping of metal on metal. Tim's eyes widen as another flew past, and before he can think Andy is the one who exclaims, "Shit! They're shooting at us!"

Tim shoves Kensington into the back of the van and hustles in, Andy clambering to shut the doors as another bullet tings against the metal. Outside the chaos escalated, people scurrying and flattening themselves behind nearby vehicles or one another. His instincts kick in through as he glances to his partner and asks, "You hit?"

Andy is pale but shakes his head, "No, you?"

Tim opens his mouth to answer when a low groan escapes Kensington. Shit. Unless it was silver all it would do is sting the man a little. "Where'd they-?" Tim stops, his eyes landing on where Kensington had been hit- his shoulder, but it wasn't a silver bullet, or a bullet at all for that matter. A tranquilizer dart jutted out of his shoulder with some dark fluid rushing like ink into the man's veins.

"Hospital," Tim blurts and bangs his fist to the partition, reinforced with silver-coated steel bars and plastic so thick with deep scratches it was impossible to see through. "We have to get him to the facility right away! Let's go Parker! DRIVE!"

The van lurches forward and the tires squeal as the rookie at the wheel gets them moving. Andy swears and settles onto the bench of the wagon, glancing anxiously at Kensington, who was laying on the metal floor moaning behind his mask, curling into fetal position. "Shit, think it's poison?" He asks with a frown.

"I don't know, but if it is we don't have time for any more games," Tim sets his eyes on Kensington's. "Come on, Kensington. Brett, just tell us who hooked you up. Repent a little. Don't let them get away with doing all this to you."

Whatever was in the dart wasn't reacting well. The mousy man trembles and breaks out into a sweat. His breathing is suddenly more labored, his anxious look even more than the one he'd expressed back in the interrogation room at the station. "He said it would work," Kensington suddenly pants, eyes large as he gazes at the empty dart sticking from his shoulder. "The serum... it was meant to control it. To stop me from losing control!"

He? Tim exchanges a glance with his partner. They were so close to getting their answer. "Who is he? Why did he set you up?"

165

"I was a fool... *ugh!*" The man suddenly cries out as seizures begin to course through him, his body reacting to whatever toxic substance was in the vial.

"Hurry, dammit!" Andy yells up at the driver and yanks out the dart before Tim can protest.

"Brett, who is 'he'?" Tim tries again, but the seizures were getting worse. He began to pray they'd make it there before it was too late, before the poison killed the werewolf.

Only the man wasn't dying. His body twisted despite the pain of the silver handcuffs and the mask and suddenly Tim gets a glimpse of Kensington's eyes glowing red like burning coals from hell.

Amidst the chaos he'd assumed someone was trying to kill the murderous man. He realized in that moment he was wrong.

"Stop! Stop the van!" An inhuman snarl suddenly escapes Kensington and Tim pounds his fist on the divider. "STOP THE VAN NOW!!!"

Kensington's body jerks and twists but already the muscles and skin warp and ripple, fur sprouting and bones cracking as they morph and shift. Andy stares, eyes round as the werewolf begins to transform, body twisting against the restraints. The handcuffs held but only for so long- the blistering skin and muscle grew against the silver-coated bonds and suddenly the metal snaps loose, freeing him. The metal mask creaks and groans but is also no match for the surge of power that came with the transformation. Kensington's snarls and moans fill the air. Worst of all the van wasn't stopping, which seriously impeded their escape. "Damn it Parker! We have a situation back here!" Andy yells up front, and suddenly Tim gets an idea.

He whips out his cell phone, speed dialing to the station for back up when the van lurches to a sudden stop, causing all three of them to lose their balance. The phone slips from his hand and as

Kensington's claw smashes down the dooming sound of plastic cracking kills the idea along with his cell phone. A low, tremulous growl comes from the werewolf- eyes flashing redder than blood or fire, the fur the same mousy brown as Kensington's with streaks of gray here and there.

Tim paused in awe despite himself. All this time dealing with monsters, yet this was the first time he'd witnessed the transformation- and the beast- up close. He waited for the moment where he'd see his life flash before his eyes, the brief time he'd had on earth like a slide show of memories. The werewolf lunged at him, but the images- cliché and wonderful – never came.

BANG!

The sound rings loud in the confines of the van, and the momentum of the massive wolf crashes over him, but it's all wrong- a spray of blood and a limp, solid mass of fur and heavy dead weight. Not the sharp teeth and claws that he'd imagined.

Tim struggles a moment, shoving the solid, limp werewolf off him. His heart was pounding and adrenaline coursed through his veins. He was covered in a spray of blood and globs of thicker things and it takes him a moment to focus his gaze.

Andy was still pointing his pistol at the werewolf's corpse, unflinching. "Like hell am I gonna stand by and let him make my partner his next meal." He snaps the safety back in place and shoves the gun back into his holster.

Tim blinks, his brain taking a moment to process what just happened. His heart felt as though it was in his throat, but he swallows and manages to cough out, "Thanks."

Andy nods but curses again, "Sonuvabitch!"

Tim could only second that thought. Their only suspect and

witness that held key evidence was lying dead at their feet.

He. So another man was behind all this mess? Well that only narrowed it down to half of the population, or less. The man they would be looking for was extremely wealthy and resourceful. Maybe they needed to revisit questioning Lucas Bane as a place to start, though Kensington himself had been well off and well connected. They had another clue but even more questions. He didn't even want to think about the paper work that this would add to his caseload.

The world had seemed to stop when Andy shot Kensington, but it dawns on Tim that the van itself had stopped too. He knocks again on the divider, which was now splattered with bits of werewolf. "Hey Parker, we're okay back here, though I think you need to revisit your driver's test."

Andy shakes his head. "Rookies," he mumbles, then adds, "You can let us out now! Pretty sure now nothing's gonna happen besides filing a bunch of paper work."

"Shots fired in public, a high profile case, and our only lead dead at our feet. More like a mountain of paper work now," murmurs Tim with a frown, shaking his hand downward and flicking off some of the blood and thicker bits to the floor of the van.

The van doors didn't open and Tim's frown deepens. Andy knocks on the front partition again. "Come on, man! McKinnon's covered in werewolf brains. I think we could both use some air."

There is still no response but the van begins moving again. Andy mutters under his breath about goddamn rookies. Tim shakes his head and attempts to wipe away some of the gore from his face, grimacing as a large, wet glob drops from his hair. "Dammit," he grumbles again, if only to keep his queasiness from rising. "That rookie better be taking us to the station or I swear I'm not just taking his badge, I'm taking his head."

14: THE CALM

Despite her almost burning need to run, to get air, and the excitement of leaving these four walls behind, Sophie had been cautious for too long to throw it all away so easily. Before they just rushed out the door she made sure to put on an inconspicuous outfit. She stared at the stranger in the mirror, an image that she had become more and more accustomed to as of late- her reflection without make up, jewelry, and her usual clothes. She realized how much more comfortable she had become. Her blonde hair was pulled back into a high ponytail, tucked under a faded Yankees ball cap and she wore one of Korban's green a-shirts with a pair of faded blue jeans. RJ's brown leather belt helped keep the rather large jeans from sliding down her hips, and a pair of Alex's running shoes completed her shabby-chic look. Someday soon she would have her own clothes again, but right now the borrowed clothes helped in more ways than one. She was pretty sure they could walk past her parents now and even they wouldn't recognize her. Satisfied she was incognito, she left Korban's bedroom and found him out in the living room.

He smiled at her in that way that reminded her that he was a man, and the admiration in his eyes made her stomach do a little flip. She smiles back in return, and the look in his amber eyes gave her a bit of satisfaction that she hadn't had in quite a while. She could smell

169

it on him too, of course, but that was a new sensation. She could sense how he wanted her, even in these borrowed clothes and without makeup he found her appealing. It had been a long time since she'd felt that kind of adoration and it gave her confidence a boost. "Ready to go?" She asks him and he nods, his yellow-gold eyes flashing with a bit of eagerness. "All right then, lead the way."

He heads to the door and opened it for her, she thanks him and the pair of them head out to the garage. On the radio heavy metal rock music is blaring. Yet even over the loud guitar riffs and crashing drums she can hear Alex humming along, the metal clanking of his tools as he worked on the car. The smells of the garage cover that enticing scent that accompanied the mechanic; oil, gasoline, metal, sweat, and burnt rubber. She tries to focus on those smells and not Alex, because for some reason he smelled like prey to her and she didn't want to repeat her loss of control again.

Korban strides over to the radio and turns the sound down, evoking a loud, "Hey!" of protest from beneath the hood of one of the cars as Alex pokes his head from around it.

"Sophie and I need to get out for a little while. I was going to see if you wanted us to pick up anything for you on the way," Korban says, a bit of mischief lighting his eyes.

"Ah, I see. Go ahead, hit the tip jar Lobo. Have a good time, don't spend it all in one place, and bring a couple six packs of something good back for later," Alex pulls out a rag from his pocket and wipes his hands, smearing oil on the already stained cloth.

"Thanks man. I owe you one," Korban picks up a mason jar filled with crumpled bills and starts to count them out on the counter.

"You owe me more than one but that's not the point," Alex winks to him then heads over to his tool box and begins rummaging around. "Just bring that beer back before dinner, I'm going to want one at closing time."

"Yes Dad," Korban teases back then flashes Sophie a playful grin as he reaches for the radio knob and switches the channel from rock to something smoother before cranking the volume back up.

"Ha! Hilarious, but I ain't even mad. I like Journey," Alex tosses the rag towards Korban and he pretends his lug wrench is a microphone and begins to belt out the ballad with Steve Perry.

Korban chuckles and scoops up the money, folding it into his pocket and then offers his hand to Sophie. She takes his hand, fingers meshing into his and offers him a relieved smile. Some of the tension melts away at his touch and as they head out the door it is like a weight is lifted from her shoulders. Korban pauses briefly to pluck out a red and blue pinwheel from along the tool wall, holding it in his free hand as they leave. A curious trinket to bring with them for sure, but something about it combined with his smile lifts her spirits.

Outside the air is filled with a symphony of scents that described the city but it was clearer, and as new scents began to fill her nostrils it was the perfect distraction. The streets are fairly empty at this time of day, only a car or two passing through the neighborhood. The sun feels warm on her skin, contrasting the cool spring breeze that carried the scent of exhaust, sweat, and a combination of other unique scents. Underneath it all was the fresh hint of spring, which promised of good things to come- green leaves and grass, fresh flowers, and new life. Beginnings that survived despite the cold grip of winter. Despite everything that had happened to her the world would continue on. Winter would melt into spring, life would find a way. As she walks up the sidewalk with her hand in Korban's, she can't help but feel the small beginning of hope that she too would make it through her own winter.

~*~

The crumbling sidewalk leads the pair from the busy streets near the garage towards a quiet residential area that begins to give way to the lush, budding trees that lined the outer edge of a park. They walk together and every step Sophie takes makes the nerves in her stomach flutter. She fears running into others, less now because of being recognized and more for what she might do. Alex had a fairly good sense of humor, but she knew a stranger may not find it too amusing if she attacked them on the street. Worse still if she bit and infected an innocent person…

She shoves away the thoughts, trying instead to focus on how nice a day it was turning out to be and how refreshing it was to breathe outdoors again. Though her senses were more human again after the full moon, her nose remained keenly on alert and picked up a variety of scents. Most dominant was Korban's scent of wolf, forest and safety with a wallop of his own nervousness. Though his smell was rooted with other blends of emotion and the heady warm, clover-like smell of his attraction to her. It made her cheeks burn when he gave her that look. Primal and intense and- her thoughts are interrupted as he suddenly releases her hand and swoops down in front of her, causing her to stop mid-step. He gracefully picks up a shiny copper coin from the sidewalk and grinning as he turns her way and extends his hand towards her, the pinwheel in his other hand spiraling wildly from his sudden movement. "Penny for your thoughts?" Korban asks as his eyes meet hers and she feels her cheeks warm under the attention of those intense golden eyes.

"Where to begin?" Sophie accepts the coin with a small smile, averting her gaze. Staring up ahead at the path as it curved towards a cluster of trees, she smirks a little in mild amusement. "I'm not sure there are enough pennies out here, or anywhere, for all the thoughts I have at the moment."

"Humor me then. How about one thought for this shiny, good luck penny?" He asks with a tilt of his head.

She chuckles and shakes her head. "All right. I suppose I can share one with you," she pauses and rubs the penny between her fingers. "I feel like you are one of the few people in this world that I can share my thoughts with, Korban. Pennies given or otherwise," He raises his eyebrows in surprise at this revelation, though Sophie smiles to him as she puts the penny in her pocket. "You are helping me through this... all of this mess. And even on this terrible day, when I was watching my own funeral not even an hour ago... you can somehow make me smile." She reaches then and takes his hand, giving it a squeeze as she begins to walk again, tugging him along with her as her words seemed to have stunned him. "I was thinking how lucky I am to have you with me, by my side."

Korban's cheeks turn a darker shade and he smiles to her, gently squeezing her hand in return. "Wow... I think I'd better find another lucky penny fast, that was certainly worth more than just one."

She giggles. "How about you tell me where we're headed, and I'll share a couple more thoughts along the way? In exchange for a few of yours, of course."

Korban grins and nods. "Sounds fair," he says, then as they turn the corner she can smell it. Barbequed chicken and pork, the scent which had been faint now fierce and causing her mouth to water. Up ahead was an elderly black woman who was stationed behind a large grill and for a moment Sophie tenses, until Korban gives her hand another squeeze. "It will be okay, I promise you. Nothing beats Maggie's barbeque, and the smell of the food will keep your wolf in check."

She squeezes his hand in return and nods, breathing in the smoky-sweet scent of the barbeque. With that came his calming scent as well. She feels the knots in her stomach loosen as they walk towards their destination. Korban periodically squeezes her hand as they approach the woman and her delightful smelling food. The woman smiles brightly and greets them warmly, introducing herself as Maggie. Korban orders up a couple specials which she served up into Styrofoam containers and wrapped them both into a plastic bag.

Sophie is barely aware of what is said, her heart pounding in her head as she concentrates on her breathing; inhaling the strong smell of the barbeque, the fresh forest scent of Korban beside her, and faintly the sweaty and spicy smell of the woman who had cooked up their lunch. She holds her breath for a moment, but instead of feeling that consuming bloodlust rise her hunger remains set on the barbeque, and to her increasing pleasure she remains in control. Whether it was her muted senses after the change or her own growing strength, it was progress. She even smiled and waved to Maggie as Korban paid for their meal, picked up the plastic sack and they headed on their way again. Her stomach gives a low growl as they continue walking along and she glances to him curiously. "So where exactly are we headed?"

"Well... I have a bit of an unconventional idea," Korban began and as they round another corner thick with trees a clearing is revealed. Green, rolling grass and stretch of land dotted with trees and various carved headstones spread out before them. Sophie raises an eyebrow to him, and he continues, "I know a picnic in the graveyard isn't probably what you had in mind but-"

"No, but it's a great idea, really," she interrupts and smiles to him. "I can't hurt anyone here. They're already dead. And hopefully staying where they are."

Korban chuckles gently. "Hopefully that is the case. The last thing we need is a zombie apocalypse."

"To add to our werewolf and vampire ridden world?" Sophie's grin widens a little at this despite herself. These boys were growing on her with their sense of humor. "Come on, let's find a spot and dig in. That barbeque smells amazing."

"I have just the place in mind," Korban says, then squeezes her hand once more and leads the way.

~*~

The sky was clear and blue as they made their way through the cemetery. A light breeze picked up just as they stopped in front of a row of headstones that were still new in appearance despite the years and weather. "Here we are," he says, depositing their lunch on a bench near a row of tombstones near a solid oak tree that towered over them. He twirls the pinwheel in his hand and smiles to Sophie. "I hope you don't mind if I pay my respects before we eat."

"No, of course I don't mind," Sophie says. "It seems the right thing to do, I mean, a cemetery is first and foremost a place to pay your respects."

He nods at that and takes a deep breath before heading over to a particular grave marking. Korban felt a new sort of nervousness in his gut as he approached his mother's grave, bending over to straighten the tipped pinwheel beneath the headstone. He brought the green and silver pinwheel the last time he'd been here to visit only a few weeks ago. He always made sure to stop by before a full moon if he could help it, if only to vent some of his frustration or pain to someone who always listened without judging him. A gentle breeze rustled through his hair and spun the green and silver plastic around in a dazzling display of color, and when he closed his eyes and inhaled deep he sometimes would catch the scent of his mother's perfume. Perhaps it was his imagination, but then again werewolves were once filed into that category too.

He cleared his throat, gazing up at the inscription on the cold stone monument. A rose was delicately etched into the grey marble, and beneath it read her name:

MARIA ANA LEIA DIEGO

BELOVED MOTHER AND DAUGHTER

"Hi Mom," he smiled, brushing some dirt away from her headstone with the pad of his thumb. He stood and gestured to Sophie, meeting her gaze as a blush crept over his cheeks. "I brought a friend with me today. Her name is Sophie."

He watched Sophie flash him a smile, then turn her attention to his mother's grave. "It is a pleasure to meet you, Mrs. Diego."

"Actually," Korban places the red and blue pinwheel into the earth on the opposite side of the headstone, balancing out the other and it too begins to lightly spin as another spring breeze rolls past, "it's Ms. Diego. My mother never married my father." He paused, glancing back to the tombstone but not really seeing it as he explained, "My father left us both a long time ago. He had a wife and a family of his own, so he didn't have time for me, or my mother after she became pregnant with me."

When he turned to her those pretty blue and gold eyes reflected an unspoken apology, but he flashed her an understanding smile. "It's okay. I don't mind. I took her last name and I'm proud to have it. My mother sacrificed so much when she had me." At the questioning tilt of her head, he added softly, "Her family kicked her out when she refused to give me up for adoption after I was born. They were deeply religious and didn't want the shame of a bastard associated with their family."

Sophie gave a soft gasp and then her warm hand was on his shoulder, gingerly touching to comfort him. He smiled, her touch was always more than welcome, even as it made his cheeks burn hotter. She was quiet for a moment, gazing to the headstone with new understanding. "You raised a good man, Ms. Diego," she whispered softly. "A wonderful man, who saved my life."

For a moment it seemed like she wanted to say more, but appeared to be at a loss for words as unspoken emotions flickered in her eyes. She turned to Korban, letting her hand drop from his shoulder and slipping her hand into his, causing his heart to flutter uncontrollably. "You are very lucky Korban, to have such amazing friends," Sophie said softly. "But I see why you do. You really are a good person."

"For a werewolf," he cracked a smile.

When he turned to her though, her expression remained serious, "No, for a man."

~*~

Back at the garage the radio was blaring, just as Alex liked it. Humming and muttering lyrics to the song he went about his work, completely lost in the moment. It was a good day for business and after this tune up he could take a break and enjoy the beautiful weather. He had both garage doors open though one port was empty, awaiting the arrival of his next appointment. The fresh air, even filtered by the city, cooled the garage with a nice breeze and caused the collection of pinwheels to spin and flutter along the wall. The tune up he was working on was going perfect. He'd have this car running better than normal in no time.

He heard a car pull into the garage and peered from the hood. His next appointment had arrived a little early, it seemed, though he could have sworn it was for an Impala, not a Durango. The S.U.V. door opened and he saw a figure from the corner of his eye. "Just a moment, sorry! Be right with you!" He called out, working quickly to finish up. Pops had taught him a lot about cars and even more about customer service. It was always best to greet your customer face to face, to keep things from becoming too impersonal.

A man's voice came. "I just need a car inspection. How long you gonna be?"

He was in good spirits, so even a rather pushy customer didn't bug him. Their money spent just as well as anyone else's. "Just a moment, please."

The customer was impatient. "I got something to take care of up the road, but I need it done today. Can I just drop it here with the keys?"

Maybe there wasn't parking and this guy was frantic, but Alex didn't mind. He'd have the guy's car keys after all. "Sure. I'll get to it after this."

"Thanks, man." Alex heard the keys jingle as they hit the counter. "Later."

"Later," he repeated then went back to finishing the tune up.

The song ended and suddenly a popular ballad blared from the stereo. Alex nearly hit his head on the hood as he hurried to change the channel. It was definitely not cool to be working on your cars with the Backstreet Boys blaring on the radio.

He wiped his hands on the rag from his back pocket and headed behind the counter to change the radio station to something with more guitars and drums in it.

He knelt down and reached for the knob and suddenly there was a loud explosion in the garage, too quick for Alex to react. The force of the blast knocked him backwards, hard into the wall. He didn't have a chance to react. His vision went red, then black.

15: THE STORM

The van wasn't stopping and as the minutes passed the blood that splattered them both became dry and itchy. With every passing minute the corner of Tim's mouth began to twitch with the force of his constant, grim frown. Andy had known his partner for a long time. They'd met in middle school and grew up on a rough side of town together, finding friendship and the arcade more appealing than joining up in a gang like many of the kids in their neighborhood. After a few years of scraping by in odd jobs after high school they decided to take the civil service exam and joined the police academy soon after. They weren't partners in the force until after the outbreak, but they'd spent many nights after their shifts hanging out at home or their favorite bar, pounding back cold ones and watching football. That wasn't including the major life events they'd shared; being one another's best man in their respective weddings, sharing a cigar after the birth of their first child, a comforting hand on a shoulder when they buried one another's parents. They knew things about one another that others didn't know, like how they preferred their coffee, what to put on and leave off on a decent sandwich, and what subtle cues meant.

Like how right now the corner of Tim's mouth was twitching along with his right pinky finger, and how that translated to his partner being astronomically pissed off. Of course, with his own temper on nuclear at the moment he really didn't have to know Tim that well to realize he was angry.

Andy gives a frustrated growl and pounds his fist on the blood and brain crusted divider for what seemed to be the hundredth time. "Parker! Goddammit you better be driving back to the station so we can shower this shit off!"

The van suddenly stopped moving, then shuddered to a halt as the keys left the ignition. "Finally," Tim grumbled, running a hand through his hair then making a face and flinging something thick from his hand to the ground, where Kensington's remains had returned to his human form and started to ripen in the van.

When the doors opened, they were outside their destination, within the familiar fenced in parking lot of Hutchings and greeted by at least a half dozen rifles pointed at them and even more officers fully geared in SWAT uniforms. "Whoa!" Tim's eyes went round in surprise and both of them wisely and slowly raised their hands in the air. "It's okay guys, we dispatched the werewolf. As you can clearly see by the mess back here."

One of the SWAT members lifted a radio to their lips and surprised them again with a female voice, "Commissioner, it looks like Sergeant McKinnon and Sergeant Ellyk are both alive. Kensington is terminated. Orders?"

The Commissioner's voice came back after a spurt of static, "I'll be right there."

For several moments the guns remained trained on them and Andy had to bite his cheek in order to keep from swearing. Tim attempted to reason with them, "Guys, is this really necessary?"

The female, the leader whose badge remained hidden by how she held her gun responded, "I'm sorry fellas, this is just protocol until the boss comes down here. You were locked in the back with that suspect and now you're covered in his blood."

"He went Wolven and he was going to kill us both!" Andy exclaimed, to which Tim gave him an imploring look that clearly meant 'shut up'.

The leader of the group frowns at this news but at that moment Commissioner DeRusso, a tall, graceful and imposing black woman in a navy pants suit emerges from the building and strides over to the van, taking one look at the bloodied sergeants and the body in the even bloodier van and cursing. "Jesus Christ, what happened here?"

The SWAT leader turns to her quickly, straightening herself. "Commissioner, we opened the van and found them like this. According to Ellyk, Kensington shifted and attacked them. They had no choice but to defend themselves."

The Commissioner swears again, shaking her head. "What the hell happened to make him shift, Ellyk? McKinnon?" She eyed them for answers.

Tim went to bat first, as he usually did. "We were under fire when we were escorting him to the van. He was hit by this dart," he gestured to the now empty dart that was sticking from Kensington's pale side, "Whatever was in it made him turn and Ellyk had to put in a bullet in him, otherwise my partner and I would have lost our lives. Andy saved my life." The look Tim gave him at that moment made it sink in to both of them, that they really had come close to the end. The look his friend and partner gave him was one that read complete and total gratitude, despite them both being covered in drying gore. They had lived to tell the tale.

"This is going to be a hell of a lot of paperwork and even more bad press," the Commissioner sighs. "Well gentlemen, I am glad both of you are alive. However, being covered in the remains of a werewolf. I'm afraid you're going to both have to spend some time getting decontaminated, and then we will have a debriefing before we go from there." She glares over to the SWAT team. "And for God's sake, stop pointing guns at my officers! They are complying with your orders and mine, the last thing I need is to lose one of my men on top of this mess."

As the SWAT team complied, Andy was gracious enough to say, "Thanks, Commissioner."

"Anytime, Ellyk. Now let's get you boys cleaned up and go over what happened again."

They had only taken a few steps when suddenly a loud, low boom in the distance sounded, almost like a random clap of thunder. It wouldn't have been strange if the sky wasn't a cloudless blue for a change. Andy saw it first. In the distance a spiraling plume of dark smoke headed up to the clear sky. "What the…?"

Heads were already turning in the direction he was staring at and a few surprised gasps filled the air. The Commissioner's cell phone began to ring and she answered it, the conversation on her end clipped and causing another frown to form on her face. When she hung up she glanced to the two of them. "First I have werewolves crashing parties and rampaging across the country side, now I have bombs going off in my city. I'm going to take care of this. Haynes and Gibson, please see that Ellyk and McKinnon are taken inside and cleaned up. I will be back later to personally talk with both of you boys about what has happened but in the meantime I have another shit storm to clean up."

"Yes ma'am," Haynes, the leader donned in SWAT gear nods then she glances to the two of them. "Let's get moving, gentlemen. I'm sure you both are more than grateful to get cleaned up. Can't be too much fun wearing werewolf remains."

Tim nods but frowns as they head towards the building, worry creasing his brow as he gives one more glance in the direction of the black smoke, but Andy can't help but feel a little relieved that whatever else was happening now wasn't their mess. At least he hoped not as he scratched off a bit of dried blood from his arm and headed into the building to get washed off.

~*~

Heading back towards the garage, Korban felt like the luckiest man alive. He'd spent the afternoon having lunch in a cemetery with the most beautiful woman in the world. Perhaps it wasn't the most traditional of dates but he had gotten her out, if only for a little while, and most importantly he helped ease her pain and made her smile. Even with dark sunglasses and her hair hidden beneath a ball cap, she still had an air of dignity and grace. He'd brought out that lovely smile that no amount of worn, casual clothes could fade. "So I have to ask," she says as they walk along, holding on to one of the six packs promised to their hard-working mechanic, "what's with the pinwheels?"

Korban smiles at that, her warm hand in his one hand and the second cold six pack in his other, "I was wondering when you would ask about that. It's a bit of a strange tradition, I know. Mom was never really one for flowers. She said it wasn't fair to kill a living thing to just enjoy it for a little while, to destroy something beautiful just to hold it captive while it wastes away. So when she was in the hospital, I wanted to bring her something, but I didn't really have a lot of money at the time, so I got her a pinwheel from the gift shop. It was the only thing I could afford, but it made her smile and she said how much she loved it. So I would bring her one, when I could, until... well, until the cancer won and took her from us all."

"It means the world to a mother, taking her words to heart and listening like that," Sophie smiles sadly, thinking of the small gestures Daniel would do for her. How much they mattered and how they mattered even more now that she couldn't be with him. She sees the pain in Korban's eyes even after losing his mother long ago, and can't help but wonder about her son, the way he looked on the television… no. She pushes the thought away for now. Korban had opened his heart and world to her, he had given her this respite during the storm. "Thank you, Korban. I don't think I'll ever be able to thank you enough," she squeezed his hand again, her fingers intertwining with his. "I'm glad that we could do this, get out for a little while. It was nice to see the city through someone else's eyes and to learn more about you."

He felt his cheeks warm at that, "I'm glad to show you around my side of town."

She opened her mouth to say something else when a loud explosion nearby rocked the ground, knocking Sophie into his arms. Both six packs rattled and crashed as they struck the pavement and from some, golden brown liquid began to bubble and pour out onto the sidewalk.

Her heart skipped two beats, and then-

"The garage!" Sophie gasped, staring up the street.

Korban turned his gaze and saw dark, billowing smoke and flames coming from the gaping maw of the garage. His eyes widened, his mouth going dry. "Alex!"

He didn't hesitate beyond that, instead sprinting at a supernatural speed towards the smoke and flames. The garage had become an inferno. He sniffed the air, fuel and metal and polyester were burning, but beyond it all he could smell Alex's blood. Sophie was calling for him but the roar of the flames muffled her cries, and beyond it all he could hear Alex's heartbeat, his pulse fluttering and weak.

He leapt over the flames and twisted metal, ignoring the wolf's protests inside of him that urged him to run back outside. The air was hot and thick with smoke. He covered his mouth with his arm and went by instinct through the dark, sweltering hell. Shuffling past pieces of metal, his lungs screamed for fresh air, but he couldn't leave Alex to this fate.

He continued forward, keeping his mouth covered and staying low. Finally he reached the counter and crawled carefully around it. He felt the rubber sole of a shoe, and then a leg. He quickly knocked away the things that had fallen on top of his friend and scooped the unconscious mechanic easily up over his shoulder into a fireman's carry. Rushing out of the garage he clung tightly to Alex. He leapt over the remains of a car, the flames licking at him as he ran. He was almost home free when he ran into a large piece of metal. With a snarl he launched the piece of metal into the wall and ran outside of the inferno, Alex slung over his shoulder.

He was a few feet away from the garage when another small explosion rang out inside the garage.

It was as if the second explosion brought everything back to life, as if the world had stopped the moments he'd been in the garage. The oxygen returned to his aching lungs, the sound of sirens filled the air, and pain flared in his leg, sticky with blood. He carried Alex, limping slightly, to where Sophie waited nearby, amidst a growing crowd of neighbors and onlookers who watched the scene with horrified wonder.

He lowered Alex to the ground as carefully as possible, not worried about his own injured leg, which had already started to heal. "Alex! Alex!!!"

Sophie knelt down beside him, her face going pale, "He's not breathing!"

There was a thud nearby and like magic RJ was there, his

briefcase abandoned on the sidewalk as he rushed over, shrugging off his jacket quickly and beginning to administer ventilations to their unconscious friend.

"Come on, Alex," Korban murmured, "you've been through worse! You can do this! Just breathe!"

The symphony of emergency vehicle sirens were getting closer, but not close enough for comfort. Korban could taste the panic and fear rolling from RJ as he frantically continued to breathe for Alex.

Alex gave a gasp, and began to cough and sputter. Korban had never heard a more beautiful sound. RJ wrapped his arms around Alex and buried his face into his best friend's shoulder, his entire body trembling. "Thank God you're alive!" He sobbed into Alex's smoke saturated shirt.

The mechanic's breaths came in gasps between coughs and his brown eyes were bloodshot when he opened them, blinking and gazing around slowly, cheeks flushed under smudges of soot. For a moment he simply gazes to them in a daze as he catches his breath. Alex's voice was raspy and weak as he manages to smile, breathing in gulping, hungry breaths. "I'll never say another bad thing about boy bands again."

Korban smirks and a chuckle escapes him, relief coursing through him and causing him to shake his head. "He's going to be just fine." If Alex was able to crack jokes, especially random ones, he had to be okay.

The wail of sirens grew nearer and RJ jerked his head towards Korban, "You guys aren't going to be, if you stick around when the police show up. You and Sophie need to get out of here. Fast." Korban swears. His roommate, the teacher, is right again. He apparently takes too long to get into motion because RJ urges him again, "Go, get out of here! Both of you! Hurry!"

Korban nods and both of the werewolves get on their feet. "Meet you at the hospital?"

"Yes, yes if it's safe. Just go, they're almost here! We can't have her cover blown now. Get lost!" RJ waves them away, and Korban catches Alex giving a small wave, then wincing at the movement.

Sophie grabs Korban's arm and the two begin to sprint down the street, heading back the way they came. They don't slow their pace until they have put a few blocks behind them and even then they slow to a jog. They keep a steady pace until they are once more on the fringes of the neighborhood, not far from the cemetery. They duck into a wooded area to catch their breath and it is then that Korban realizes Sophie is shaking, her hand still gripping his arm. He gazes to her, turning to face her and putting his free hand gently over her white-knuckled one. "Sophie-"

She cuts him off by grabbing him, pulling him to her. Then her lips meet his, crushing his mouth to hers. Her arms wrapped around him, fingers pressing into his skin and urging him closer against her. He wraps his arms around her as he returns her kiss until she releases him, breathless, the worry still reflected in her bright blue eyes. "If you ever scare me like that again, Korban Diego, so help me I swear I'll-" He cuts her off this time, capturing her lips again and as she melts against him they both lose a few more minutes of time, tension easing away as they kissed.

When they tenderly pull away her gaze locks on his and she whispers, "When you ran into the garage like that… when I couldn't see you in the smoke and flames…" She runs her hands along the sides of his face, raw fear in her eyes for a brief moment and then relief reflecting in those sky blue pools. "I couldn't breathe, not until I saw you come out of there with Alex," her gaze lowers to inspect his leg and his eyes follow hers. There was a long tear in his jeans, the rip itself singed and bloodied but the skin underneath was healing, a jagged scab that was slowly vanishing, skin stitching back together again before their eyes like an odd time lapse. "Are you going to be okay? Should a doctor look at that?"

"I'll be all right," Korban gives her a smile, her concern filling him with contentment. The adrenaline rush was wearing off now but thankfully his rapid healing was dulling the deep ache of his wounded shin. "We should head to the hospital and make sure that Alex is too. Maybe he can shine some light on what the hell happened at the garage to cause that explosion."

As they started their walk towards civilization Sophie took his hand again. "Do you think it was some terrible accident? Maybe a mistake was made, a wire crossed with gasoline or something like that?"

Korban frowns, shaking his head. "No, I don't think so. Alex knows cars inside and out, he's been working on them with Pops since he was barely out of diapers. There's no way he'd make a mistake that would cause something that big to happen…" He trails off, but Sophie did bring up the frightening question.

If it wasn't a mistake, then who exactly caused the explosion?

16: RECOVERY

RJ was pacing anxiously in the waiting room when they arrived at the hospital, easily out lapping any of the expectant fathers there. Korban watched him, his nose burning with the foul combination of antiseptic and blood, of sickness and worry that permeated through the waiting room. He felt his own wolf pacing within him, wanting to check on their fallen pack mate. "RJ, how is he?" Korban blurted as he approached his friend, Sophie keeping close to his side.

RJ paused his patrol and turned his worried gaze to them. His was wringing his hands and fidgeting, the strong emotions rolling off him in a scent more pungent than the lingering smoke on his clothes. "I don't know, I've been waiting out here since the ambulance brought us here. They took him right in to take care of his burns and to check him for internal injuries. I've been out here waiting since." He gestured to Korban's torn pant leg and asks, "Are you all right?"

"I'm fine, really. It healed up on the walk over," Korban barely felt the dull throb in his leg any more, his concern focused on their wounded friend.

"Good, good," RJ nods and resumes his pacing. "Alex is going to be okay. He has to be."

"He's been through a lot, he's tough, he will be," Korban agreed and hoped.

"You both saved his life back there," Sophie adds, offering a smile to RJ. "He is alive because of both of you, I'm sure he'll pull through."

A couple people in the waiting room glanced over at the trio and some got up and moved away, the scent of their apprehension spiking in the air. For a brief moment Korban was confused by their looks aimed his way, then he realized he hadn't worn his sunglasses to cover his eyes. He shifts his gaze to Sophie, who kept a firm grip on his hand. Her nostrils were flaring, scenting the fear in the people there, and for a moment the feral look in her eyes makes him wonder if maybe they should step outside. But she doesn't make a move to chase any of them down and catching his glance she supplies, "I am good, I just don't like how they keep looking at you like that."

His stomach does a happy little flip at her words and a smile curves his mouth despite those scrutinizing stares. RJ pulled out his phone and glanced at it, most likely to check the time, and it dawns on Korban. "RJ, mind if I borrow your phone for a moment? I should check and see if I can get a hold of Tim and fill him in on what happened." If Sergeant McKinnon had heard about the explosion by now, he would be trying to get a hold of Korban or RJ. It would be best to beat him to the punch.

"Sure, yeah, of course," RJ hands over the device and Korban accepts it, putting a hand on the teacher's shoulder and giving it a comforting squeeze.

"Alex will be okay," Korban emphasizes, meeting RJ's eyes despite his inner wolf's protests, which were weak at best thanks to being sated after the full moon.

RJ nods again, some of the tension leaving him for a moment.

Korban already knew that it wouldn't be until he laid eyes on Alex that he would truly relax, but he had to try.

He checks the display screen on the phone but so far Tim hadn't called, which could be good or bad. Korban dials the phone number from memory, and frowns as it goes right to Tim's voice mail. As the familiar recording recites instructions Korban murmurs, "Still not answering his phone… I hope everything is okay." He decides to leave another message, and when prompted he joins RJ in his pacing. "Hey, Tim, it's Korban again. I hope everything is okay, and whatever has you away from the phone isn't too big a crisis. Not that you can't handle it," he pauses for a moment. "I don't know if you heard by now or not, but there was an explosion at the garage. Alex is hurt and we're all camped at Saint Joseph's Hospital waiting to see him. When you get this please give me a call. On RJ's phone, mine was left at the apartment and I don't really know if it survived the blast." For the first time it dawned on him, that cold feeling in his stomach. Their den, their home, had been violated. It made him nauseous. "Please call when you get this." He rattled off RJ's phone number just in case then hung up and handed the phone back to RJ.

They waited anxiously for the next few hours for news on Alex's condition. Thankfully the waiting room was quiet that day, and most who did glance their way seemed to look away rather quickly once they caught sight of Korban's wolfish eyes. It was one of the few times he was thankful for his difference, though, as they didn't linger long on Sophie to figure out who she was. Hiding in plain sight, who would have thought it would be this easy?

Sophie kept her hand in his most of the time they sat there, which kept him from climbing the walls. RJ took turns pacing and sitting alongside them, until the past hour, which he remained sitting, having exhausted himself. He glanced periodically at his phone, but Sergeant McKinnon had yet to return their calls. Korban hoped again that he was having a better day than they were, but chances were if he hadn't returned his calls Tim was most likely just as busy if not more so than they had been.

When a female doctor finally approached in a white lab coat over green scrubs RJ was the first one on his feet when she called, "Mister Ramirez?"

"That's me," RJ rushes over, not having to be called twice. "How is Alejandro?"

"He's awake and asking for you. We have him settled in recovery and I can take you to him now, if you'll follow me," she offered a kind smile.

"Yes, please," the relief was palpable in RJ's body language and the three of them follow the doctor to Alex's room. RJ was the first in the door, thanking the doctor as he brushed past her. Korban and Sophie followed him inside and the doctor lingered in the doorway, watching them but their eyes were all on their friend.

Alex was out of his burnt and smoky clothes and his left arm was neatly bandaged, an oxygen tube in his nose and an IV connected to his right arm. He grinned to them, looking beyond exhausted, propped up by his elevated hospital bed. "Hey," he croaked, his voice still hoarse and his eyes red, but his smile was as bright as always.

Korban smiled as relief flooded the room, most of all coming from RJ, who took a seat closest to his best friend. "Hey," RJ said, obviously struggling to keep from breaking down, his voice wavering with emotion, "how you feeling?"

"Eh, I've been better," Alex managed a grimace. "I know how it feels to be barbequed now. Can't say it's pleasant, but they gave me magic medicine that make it not so bad," he coughed, then his eyes went from RJ to Korban. "You got me out of there, Lobo. You saved my life."

Korban smiled at that and moved closer to his friend's bedside as Sophie lingered by the window. "Yeah, but don't make me regret it later, okay?"

Alex chuckled at that, which spurred another round of coughing. His eyes were bright with amusement as his breathing evened out, "You'd get bored without me around. Don't deny it."

"Thankfully we don't know the answer to that," Korban counters.

RJ takes Alex's good hand in his and squeezes it, his dark brown eyes watery and glistening with unshed tears. Relief etched in his smile, until worry tugged at the brief happiness there. "Do you remember what happened?"

Alex frowned thoughtfully for a moment, his hand remaining in RJ's. "I was going over to change the radio station behind the counter, and I heard a really loud noise," his frown deepens and he gives a slow shake of his head, wincing and lifting his bandaged hand up to rub his temple. "That's all I remember."

The doctor chimes in, "Take your time, Mister Cyrus," she says as she approaches his bed, checking the different monitors and things that Alex was connected to and jotting down notes on her clipboard. "All things considered, you are doing pretty well for a man who was in a close range explosion. You are lucky to have gotten out of there when you did, and more importantly that you weren't hit by much shrapnel from the blast. Either the fall or the force of it broke your arm, but we have that set now and we'll be monitoring you overnight just as a precaution from the smoke inhalation. It looks like the CT scan on your head is normal too, just a bad bump to the head and no hemorrhaging. All good signs."

"You hear that?" Alex grins. "The doctor says I'm normal!"

"Well, she doesn't know you as well as we do," Korban

cracks, and they laugh until Alex's laughter turns into another coughing fit.

"I'll go put the paperwork in and they'll be bringing you some more pain killers. If you need anything in the meantime, the nurse is a button push away," the doctor gestures to the call button connected to his bed and then leaves the room, an amused smile on her lips.

"Thanks Doc," Alex murmured as she parted ways. He was grinning again, though the effort made him look exhausted, or perhaps it was the pain killers finally setting in. "What a day. My two best friends saved my life. Literally pull me out of the fire." His smile wavers and tears begin to stream down his cheeks. "I can't believe it. Pops' garage. Our home, it's gone. It's all gone." He broke into a fit of heartbreaking sobs, scrubbing at his face with his bandaged hand but the tears continued to flow.

RJ wraps an arm around Alex as best as he can, trying to comfort him but unable to give a proper hug due to all the cords and wires connected to the mechanic. "We don't know that, the firemen got there pretty fast, they were putting out the fire when we left there."

"Pops would be so pissed at me," Alex shook his head, choking on another sob and a funny whistling noise leaving him as he sniffled into the oxygen tube on his nose. "Not only getting the garage blown up, but breaking his cardinal rule. Always greet the customer. Lucky the last guy who came by wasn't hurt too in the blast... was he?"

RJ exchanged a glance with Korban. "You see anyone leave the garage? You guys got there a little before I did."

"No," Korban said, though that icy feeling had returned in his gut.

"I didn't see anyone either," Sophie murmured, gazing

worriedly to Alex.

"This guy, the last customer you had before the explosion, did he say anything to you? Did you see him?" RJ gently asked.

"No, no I was under the hood of another car, the guy was in a hurry," Alex's face scrunches up in frustration at the memory. He hiccups and attempts a shaky breath, his lungs still rasping on the remnants of smoke inside of them. "He tossed his keys on the counter, left his car with me. Black Durango that needed a car inspection."

RJ frowned. "Did he have an appointment?"

Alex coughs. "Yes. No. Not sure," his tears seemed to stop for now, his upset turning to confusion as exhaustion set in. His eyelids suddenly seemed to droop as he explained in a weary voice, "I was expecting an Impala. Not a Durango. He didn't even give his name and left the car. I should've greeted him. Pops would be so angry."

By the time he finished talking it looked like Alex was going to burst into tears of regret once more, but miraculously the medicine kicked in, and with a final soft sigh Alex dozes off, the mechanical sound of the oxygen tank puffing in time with his raspy, light snoring.

Watching Alex sleep, RJ said what was going through all their minds, though no one had wanted to admit it a loud yet. "This was no accident," his voice held a dangerous growl to it that made Korban's wolf proud.

Korban nodded grimly. "Alex took precious care in every car he serviced. There was no way this was caused by any sort of negligence on his part. That guy left his car and ran off in time to escape the explosion."

Sophie looked away from Alex's pale, bandaged form and stared out the window. She wrapped her arms around herself. "They found out I was hiding there, they must have tried to kill me again. I put all of you in danger."

"No-" Korban began, but RJ interrupted.

"No, Sophie. I don't blame you for this and neither does Alex. We knew the risks of helping you. No one could predict this."

Sophie nodded grimly. "I know that but," she looked to them, "you're the first real friends I've had in a long time. I don't want to be the reason I lose you."

"You won't lose us," Korban walked over to her, putting his hands on her trembling shoulders. Almost instantly she relaxed, leaning into his touch. "We're seeing this through together."

RJ nodded when she glanced to him. "We must have discovered too much. They attacked our home. They put Alex in this hospital bed. They tried to put us all in an early grave. This is more than personal now."

"They poked the wrong werewolves," Korban growls and her eyes lock with his. "I won't let them take you. No. We won't let them take you. We're a Pack now. Whoever thought they'd get away with blowing up our den, of trying to kill us... they're going to wish they had by the time we are through with them."

~*~

By the time they had turned in their bloody clothes and weapons in to evidence, had gone through the events multiple times with the county sheriff's office, and finally taken hot showers to be finally free of the sticky, dried gore, both Tim and Andy were more than happy to put this day behind them. Tim was grateful when they could finally step out of the stuffy interrogation room and out into the hall. The donuts in the lobby were stale but the coffee was fresh, and it simply felt good just to be done with it all.

As they signed out and stepped out into the cool night air, like a miracle Patty appeared, pulling up in her pale green Cadillac. Tim sank into the front seat, feeling even more relieved than when he'd stepped into the shower a few hours before. Inside the car they were greeted by the sweet and savory smell of Chinese take-out and he realized he couldn't remember his last meal. As she handed paper bags of food to both of them Tim could have cried with joy. "Patty, you really, truly are an angel," Andy read his mind, saying the words before he could.

Patty smiled, looking relieved to set eyes on the two of them. "I'm just glad you boys are all right. When I heard about the shots fired at the van, and you both being trapped in there with a werewolf..." She shudders at the memory, trailing off. "I called your wives to let them know you are both okay. I told them I'd make sure you both went home with full bellies so I picked up some take out at Rong Cheng."

"You truly are our office goddess," Tim accepts his bag. "Thanks, I hope Donna wasn't too worried."

"She's better now. At least she was when I last talked to her, letting her know that you both would be getting out of here. I think she was concerned that you'd check in but not check out, especially since you were both trapped in that van with a lycanthrope." She eyed them both again. "You are really okay, right?"

"Yeah, we've been poked and prodded and examined and interrogated enough for one lifetime," Andy unceremoniously dug into the paper bag and retrieved a wrapped eggroll, practically tearing into it even through the wax paper wrapping. "Mmm," he paused to swallow then added, "we're clean. No quarantine for us, thank the powers that be."

"Well, I'm happy to hear that. It wouldn't be the same at the office without you two around," Patty smiles, then her expression changes as something dawns on her and she turns to Tim. "Your phone was destroyed, wasn't it? It seems that a few messages were forwarded to the office. It's been crazy there so I wasn't able to get to the phone every time it rang, but if you want to check your messages on my phone you can."

"Thanks, I think I may take you up on that." Most of the calls were probably from his wife, frantic that he hadn't checked in with her after several hours of unread text messages. After listening to a few of the messages though, he swallows a bite of his own eggroll and curses under his breath. "Korban's been trying to get a hold of me, and apparently he's at Saint Joe's because Alex was hurt in that explosion. We should stop by there on our way back and check up on them."

"Sure thing," Patty turns the boat of a car towards the hospital as they continue to dig in to their dinner.

"One last stop, then we'll be homeward bound," Tim vows to himself as much as his partner, who nods in resignation.

"Well, shit," Andy sighs but polishes off his egg roll and pulls out a paper box teeming with beef lo mein, "now you've gone and jinxed it."

~*~

His words lingered with her as she watched them later that evening. RJ had fallen asleep in the chair he pulled over next to Alex's bedside, and Korban had dozed off against the corner of the room. She knew they didn't blame her for this but it tore at her heart anyway, knowing she'd cost them their home and almost Alex's life.

She felt suddenly choked up and needed some air. She got up and wandered the hospital halls, which seemed to constrict around her, making her queasy. Or maybe it was the combination of guilt and the industrial smell of chemical-coated sickness that lingered everywhere.

She went outside of the hospital and walked around, sucking in a great lung full of fresh air. The smells of the city were more than welcome to her nostrils. Above her the sky was darkening, the incoming twilight revealing the display of stars and the shrinking moon, still dimmed by the glow on the horizon.

She had to warn Nikki, it dawned on her suddenly. They attacked her friends, surely her sister was in danger. She spotted a nearby pay phone, thankful that the relic still existed at this hospital as she begins dialing Nikki's number collect.

After a few rings, her sister picked up, "Nikki Winters."

"Nikki, it's me," Sophie said quickly, her voice choking up with emotion, "I need to talk to you."

There was silence on the other line, and for a long moment Sophie wondered if Nikki's cell phone had dropped out. Then, "Sissy? What is it? What's wrong?"

"They found me again, Nikki. They bombed the garage, and nearly killed Alex. If I had been there..." She trembled at the thought. What had happened was already bad enough.

"Oh God, Sophie! Where are you?" Nikki asked. "Are you okay? Do you want me to come there?"

"No," Sophie blurted, unable to fight back her tears any longer, "no, Nikki. I need you to take Danny, and you both need to go. Get out of Syracuse. Before... before something else happens."

"Sissy-"

"Nikki, there isn't time! You need to get Daniel and leave tonight. Please do this for me. I want to know that you're both safe. I don't think I could handle it if something bad happens to both of you too!" She sagged against the brick wall of the building. "Especially because of me."

"Sophie," Nikki tried again, her voice softer this time. "Sophie, you know I can't just grab Daniel and shuttle him off to the airport. They have laws, and security. I don't have the same last name, without documentation they won't let him step foot out of the airport, especially for a red eye flight."

Sophie felt a wave of hopelessness crash over her at Nikki's words, the reality of the situation weighing heavily on her heart. "Then take a car, Nikki. Take a train or a bus! I don't care what you have to do, but you have to get yourselves out of here tonight!" Silence on the other line again, and for a split second Sophie wondered again if the cell phone had dropped the call, and her grip nearly cracked the plastic shell of the payphone. "Nikki?!"

"I'm here, just thinking Sissy," Sophie could hear the clicking of Nikki's heels on the floor and could see her sister pacing in her mind's eye. She could hear the squeak of them as she came to a sudden stop. "Wait, I'm a genius. If you left temporary custody of Daniel to me, I could easily get him on the jet and we could be out of here in no time."

Her heart soared with renewed hope. "You think so?"

"I know so! It'd be simple, really. I could meet up with you, just briefly, and get your signature on a letter saying you allow Daniel to fly with me. The airlines won't have the liability if I give them your signature giving the okay. They won't think twice to let him fly out of town with me!"

Sophie frowned thoughtfully. "I don't know. It's not safe to be around me right now, Nikki." Once again she thought of the way she'd pounced on Alex and bit her bottom lip worriedly.

"Sissy, it won't take that long. I'll hand you the paper, you sign it,

I go get Daniel and fly away before the night is up," Nikki sighed. "Look, Sissy, if you're right about this we don't have much time to discuss it. We need to move, now."

Sophie bit her bottom lip, then brought her hand to her mouth and chewed at her nails, something she hadn't done in a very long time. Nikki was right, though she feared what she might be capable of doing to her sister. Still, it was the only chance that both her sister and her son could get out of town and to safely, before the news travelled that she had survived the explosion. An amazing idea struck her and suddenly she was able to think straight again. "Remember where we put Nana's memorial last spring?"

"Of course I do. The Butterfly Garden of Hope, on one of the benches by the lake," Nikki said matter-of-factly.

"Good. Meet me there in a half hour," Sophie instructed. "Just promise me, Nikki. I sign the papers and you leave to get Danny right away. It really is not safe to be around me right now."

"It won't take long Sissy. You be careful too," Nikki pleaded, pausing only briefly before adding, "See you soon."

"I love you, Nikki. Thank you for doing this," Sophie felt so relieved, knowing that in only a few short minutes from now her family would be safely out of harm's way.

"Love you too, Sissy."

The phone line clicked and a dial tone hummed from the phone. Sophie set the receiver on the cradle and for a moment just breathed, leaning against the solid, cool wall of the hospital. She dreaded returning inside, but there was one last thing she wanted to do inside before she went down to meet with her sister.

She held her breath as long as possible as she walked back through the stuffy halls, taking the stairs back up to Alex's room. The nurses on the floor didn't pay her any mind as she walked past them, busy with their important tasks. She stepped in the doorway and finally breathed normally again. Here was her new family, her dear friends' scents familiar and safe to her.

There still was the residual smell of smoke on Alex's oil and gasoline scent, and sweat along with RJ's chalk and paper like smell. She watched the three of them resting, her eyes lingering on Korban. His scent was still like the forest, her sanctuary. Only even mingled in his woodsy odor she found a reminder of the flame and smoke he'd barreled through in order to save Alex's life.

She would not put them in any more danger. Nikki and Daniel would soon be out of harm's way, it was only best if she did the same for her dear friends. Especially Korban, who made her heartache as she watched him sleep there, still propped up against the corner of the room. He had suffered so much already, she wouldn't be the cause of his suffering any longer.

She bit her bottom lip again, finding it more difficult to tear her eyes away from him than she ever could imagine. "Good bye," she whispered under her breath, and then turned and darted back out of the hospital and into the night.

~*~

They arrive at the hospital, weary but in better spirits now that they had food in their bellies and an end in sight to their long and arduous day. "Good evening," Tim flashed his badge along with Andy to the attendant at the front desk. "Sergeants McKinnon and Ellyk. We're here to visit a guest of one of your patients, Alejandro Cyrus."

"No problem, officers," the young woman began typing into her computer and scanned the screen. "Just one moment while it loads."

"Hey Tim," Andy jabs his partner suddenly and gestures with

the same finger towards the exit doors. "There he goes now."

Tim turns and spies their charge hurriedly making his way outside. "Thanks," he tells the hospital employee, then hurries after Korban to catch up, calling out his name, "Korban! Diego! Hey, hold up!"

The last statement catches his attention as Korban freezes and turns to face them. The normally on edge werewolf seemed extra anxious, but given the circumstances Tim could understand. Even as they approached there was a look of worry that only seemed to deepen. "Tim. Sergeant McKinnon," Korban corrects himself, another sign that things weren't right, "I have so much I need to tell you."

"Clearly, based on the messages you left. Take a breath, man. Let's go outside and talk. We've both had long days." Tim claps his shoulder and he can feel the tension singing through him.

Korban nods, his gaze darting for the door. "Sure. Yeah." His nostrils were flaring and Tim could only imagine that the scents of the hospital were probably most uncomfortable to his friend, and going outside would be a great relief.

As they step outside, Korban's eyes continue to frantically search around. For what, or who, remains unclear. Of course, his home had been bombed, and that was more than enough to make anyone nervous, especially a territorial werewolf. They walk along, Korban leading the way, pacing at first then moving towards the parking lot. "Hey, man, if you're worried about the law and restrictions don't. We can figure something out for you until the garage is repaired. Lucky thing, the full moon was just the other day so it may not even be an issue. They won't revoke RJ's right to be your handler, I'll see to it personally. Your tip about Brett Kensington wanting to pay to be bitten was a great help to our investigation in the Sophie Bane case and you've been an upstanding citizen so…" Tim trails off, hoping his speech had placated some of Korban's worries, but instead it seemed an older, more familiar look took the worry from his expression- guilt.

Korban pauses, and his head hangs down. "Sophie..."

"There's nothing you could have done," Tim begins, but the werewolf's golden eyes meet his and he forgets his words.

"That's the thing, Tim. I did plenty to help her. I just... there's no time to explain. She needs your help, our help. Before it's too late. We need to find her, she's trying to protect us but she's putting herself back in the crosshairs." Korban sniffs the air. "I'm pretty sure I have her trail and can follow it. We need to hurry before-"

"Korban, you're not making any sense," Tim scratches the side of his beard, frowning. "Who are you talking about?"

Those amber eyes of a predator were filled with desperation. "Sophie is alive, at least she is for now. Please, please trust me that we don't have time to go into it all, but I promise you once she is safe I will tell you everything. We will tell you every bit of it together. But if we don't find her soon, I'm afraid she'll be- it will be too late."

Tim blinks, exchanging a glance with his stunned partner, then looks to the werewolf again. It's a split second decision, made by his instincts and years of knowing Korban.

As Andy and him climb into the car and instruct Patty to follow Korban, who races after Sophie Bane's scent, Andy curses under his breath. "Should have known that our night was only beginning."

17: MONSTER

The park was thankfully empty when she arrived. Only a few cars whizzed by on the nearby parkway at this time of night. It was dark, with only a few solar-powered lanterns dimly lighting the way along the memorial's sidewalk. Sophie paced along the winding path that lead from a wooden gazebo through some tall, shady bushes that would soon be bursting with flowers. She stared down at the names engraved on the bricks beneath her feet as she walked, flinching and anxiously glancing up at every car that passed.

She ducked through some low hanging branches near the end of the short path and walked over to the bench closest to Onondaga Lake. She remembered being here just about a year ago surrounded by her family; her parents, her grandfather, Nikki, Lucas and Daniel all together on a lovely spring day when it was unseasonably warm and sunny out for Syracuse. The Butterfly Garden was in full bloom and true to its name sake the butterflies fluttered around, pausing to drink nectar from the brightly colored flowers. The shiny butterfly-shaped name plate was in memory to her Nana and it glistened now even in the shadows of night fall. Sophie sat down on the bench and carefully wiped the dirt from the copper-colored plate and for a few moments just breathed.

The smells around here were abundant, which was one reason she chose this location. The lake itself had the strong smell of fish and chemicals, pollution embedded deep into the lake bed from years ago, when the world was a lot less eco-friendly. Then there was the car exhaust from the parkway and the highway on the other side of the lake, and the not too distant and wonderful smell of hotdogs grilling at Heid's. The fresh, clean scent of the green grass and the flowers that were ready to bloom any day now. Her nose could even detect the final remnants of salt from the last of winter's sludge, near the side of the road. These were all welcome distractions to her sensitive nose. She did not want to smell her sister as prey and attack her like she had Alex.

A frog croaks and she jumps at the unexpected loudness of it, watching as it leaps with a splash into the lake. Her heart was racing and she felt the urge to run. She took deep breaths, retaking in all those different scents and sounds. The wind picked up and she could smell the forest, the pine and musky scent that reminded her of Korban. She relaxed. Until she heard a branch snap and she jumped, turning around in the direction the noise had come from.

A shadowy figure stood at the end of the path, illuminated by the small glowing lanterns on the other side of the bushes and trees. She jumped back again, until the figure came into focus in the moonlight and she heard his voice, "Sophie."

Relief filled her, quickly followed by a new kind of anxiety. "Korban," she rushed over to where he stood, "what are you doing here?"

"I could ask you the same thing," Korban says, looking hurt. Sophie frowns, renewed guilt gnawing at her gut. She did feel awful about sneaking off in the middle of the night after all he and the others had done for her, but it was the only way. She had to make him understand. Her heart broke when he asked, "Why did you run away?"

"I can't stick around and put you guys in any more danger," Sophie felt tears prickle in her eyes. "I'm sorry Korban, I am so grateful for everything you have done for me. There is no way I can ever thank you enough for all you've sacrificed for my safety. But now I must do the same for you. The only way I can protect you is to leave you out of this, leave everyone out of this." She sucked in a deep breath, "Nikki is meeting me here before she takes Daniel out of Syracuse."

"What?" Korban's eyes widened, his face falling. "Nikki knows that you're alive?"

"I had to warn her, to get her and Danny to safety, Korban. I can't stand by any more. Not when those I love are in danger," Sophie met his eyes, and in the pain she saw in those amber orbs, she saw that light she'd come to know. "I have to face Lucas, alone. I wanted to make sure that the people I care about were safe first."

"Sophie I don't-" Before he could further protest a car pulled off the parkway, the headlights beaming through the darkness of the garden and growing brighter as the vehicle approached them, coming to a stop at the edge of the gravel parking lot. There it stopped, but the bright lights remained on them like a spotlight.

"That's her," Sophie gazes back to Korban, chin held high, her determination to protect him, their friends and the ones she loves stronger than the other conflicting feelings that swarmed her. She walks towards the car as the doors to the SUV open. The familiar scent of her sister's favorite perfume eases the knot in her stomach. "Nikki, thank God you're safe."

Her sister steps out of the passenger side and flashes her a dazzling smile. "Sissy, I wish I could say the same to you."

There is a menacing metallic click to her right, but it's Nikki's words that make Sophie freeze in place. The moment is so surreal that even after all the odd events of that day she couldn't process what was happening. One of Lucas' bodyguards, Matt, was standing outside of the driver's side of the car with an odd looking gun pointed at her. Nikki had a triumphant smirk that twisted her lovely, photogenic smile into something cold, cruel, and unrecognizable. "Nikki… what…?"

Korban growls from behind her, and Nikki clucks her tongue. She waggled a finger at them. "Uh-uh. I wouldn't test Matt's skills with that weapon. He's a damn good shot. So I suggest you stay put and don't try to play hero, again. You've already gotten in my way too many times Wolfman." Her eyes narrow and she glares from him back to Sophie. "Though you haven't gotten in my way nearly as much as my dear, sweet older sister has so I can forgive you as long as you don't do anything stupid now."

Sophie's mind spun in confusion at her sister's words. Part of her understood every word, another part was trying desperately to deny them. "What are you talking about Nikki?" She asked, unable to keep the emotion from cracking her voice.

"Don't act so innocent," Nikki rolled her eyes and glanced to Matt. "If they try anything, shoot them both." She doesn't step around the car but folds her arms over her chest as she gazed coldly to her sister. "You should have just listened to me before. But no, instead you had to be the pious one, the one who stayed despite all the evidence Lucas was a cheating bastard. You refused to budge, wouldn't leave him. So I had to make you go."

She can't stop the tears from spilling over any longer. "All of this… is because of you? You planned for that monster to kill me?"

"Unfortunately Kensington was sloppy, but it seems he did at least manage to infect you. Which makes what comes next easy," Nikki nods to Matt, whose gun clicks again. "That tranquilizer gun contains a special toxin that triggers the transformation without a full moon. You can't keep getting in my way if you go Wolven and never turn back."

Nikki's cruel words sink in, each cold word like a knife in her heart. "Nikki, please…" She takes a step toward her, and Matt points the menacing weapon towards her head, causing her to freeze in place, wet tears streaming down her face. She doesn't reach to wipe them away.

Nikki only keeps that plastic smile on display, putting a hand up to halt Matt. "Wait. I think I'll allow her a couple last words. I'm not a completely heartless bitch, after all," she tilts her head then gives a tittering laugh, "though after the toxin enters you, I guess you will be, Sissy."

Sophie opens her mouth to speak but a choking sob escapes her, the betrayal of her own sister- who had been sleeping with her husband, and was behind the unthinkable- too much to bear. "Sophie," Korban's voice starts and he moves toward her, concern etched on his face.

Matt moves the gun swiftly, barking out, "Don't move!"

Through her tears Sophie can see Korban's bright yellow eyes narrow and he growls, "How could you do this to her? Your own sister?"

"No one gets in my way when I want something," Nikki's voice remains flat and cold, sending chills through her, "not even my dear, sweet sister. Lucas may have married her, but it's me he wants. Once she's out of the way he'll be mine." She pauses. "No one gets in my way," she repeats, then motions to Matt. "Shoot him first. We don't have time for games. Or witnesses."

Sophie's eyes widen as Matt aims the strange gun at Korban. She doesn't think, only reacts as the bodyguard pulls the trigger. Leaping at a speed she didn't realize she was capable of, she moves in front of Korban just in time, and feels the sharp stab of the shot as it strikes the center of her chest. Korban's voice comes from behind her, pained and disbelieving, "No! Sophie!"

She watches the dart, sticking out of her body, a dark liquid entering her, and not even seconds later a burning sensation coursing through her veins, causing her to scream and curl into fetal position. Korban's arms are around her before she hits the ground. The toxin that Nikki had referred to felt like boiling acid in her blood, the pain triggering something even more primal inside of her, and as Korban yanks out the dart from her chest she realizes it is too late. Already her body is burning up, and inside her wolf is beginning to claw her way up to the surface.

She's only vaguely aware of what Nikki is saying as she retreats back into the SUV with Matt, who keeps the dart gun leveled on Korban. "Let's go… as much as I want to watch this, I think we better go before she draws attention over here…"

"What about the Wolfman?" Matt asks, still eyeing him through his scope.

"Shoot-" Nikki begins, but Sophie's screams seemed to have drawn the attention of a passerby and a pale Cadillac suddenly rolls off the parkway and zooms towards them.

Matt's finger is on the trigger but his head jerks towards the new threat and he fires his weapon as he moves into the driver's seat. The tranquilizer gun clicks and something whizzes past her ear with a whistle, before striking its target with a wet thud. Sophie gasps, fear for Korban fueling her anger as another ripple of pain tears a scream from her throat. Nikki quickly ducks back into the SUV, shielding her face from the headlights, Matt already revving up the engine.

Another yell tears through her as the transformation begins to take hold of her, causing her body to thrash against Korban. She can't believe this- all of this was because of Nikki. The pain of her betrayal was suddenly engulfed with the rage of the beast within her. She fights back another cry, emitting a howl of rage as fur begins to sprout, bones snap and reposition.

"Sophie, hang on! You have to fight it! We can fight this together!" Korban pleads, pain in his voice, and as he hovers over her she can see tears in his beautiful yellow eyes.

"Korban-" Sophie begins through gritted teeth. She wants to tell him so much more in that moment, before the transformation overcomes both of them, but words escape her as a blinding, burning pain rips another howl from her lips. She reaches up with a trembling hand, her fingernails already sprouting claws, but she caresses his cheek as the tears begin to fall freely down. There are worried shouts, voices from the car that had pulled over, but she can no longer understand them, and they no longer matter. All that matters is the change, spurred by her thirst for revenge on her sister for all she had done to her and now Korban too. Everything seems to slow down and speed up at the same time as the toxin-triggered transformation finishes, her final thought something that the beast agrees with before she completely takes over.

Nikki will pay for this.

~*~

"Korban! What the hell is going on here?!" Tim shouts as he opens up the car door only to stop and stare wide-eyed at the scene before them in total disbelief.

Sophie Bane was indeed alive, howling in agony as she writhed on the ground, transforming into a golden-colored wolf before their eyes as Korban attempted to calm and comfort her. The look in his eyes was equally pained as he knelt beside her. Andy curses and Patty grips the wheel in terror, crying out in surprise. This was the second transformation he'd witnessed, and it was even more horrifying. "Close the door!" Andy's voice snaps him out of it and he yanks the door closed in time for the newly turned werewolf to charge, leaping towards their car and causing Patty to squeal.

The Wolven- Sophie- blazes like a streak after the SUV that had peeled off, moving faster than Tim could ever imagine. He watches, mesmerized as Sophie catches up with the car as it spins out towards the parkway, her sharp teeth piercing one of the back tires as it turns, causing it to burst and send sparks flying. She yelps and reels back as the SUV attempts to speed away, swerving wildly to make its get away. Shaking her head, she follows the vehicle, jaws snapping as the SUV races down the parkway.

Andy bursts out from the other side of the car and cautiously approaches Korban, Tim following his partner's lead and snapping out of his temporary stupor. "Korban! Are you okay?" He asks, carefully watching as Korban stares in Sophie's direction, hunched over on his knees in the grass.

"I... I'm sorry I can't explain it all," Korban pants in a strained voice, clutching his arm, his hauntingly yellow eyes bright in the darkness. "I wanted to, I really did. I owe you that... but there's not much time now..." It is then he pulls the familiar looking dart from his arm and the now harmless, empty thing falls to rest in the damp grass. Tim's eyes widen as recognition dawns, but before he can say anything, Korban grunts, growling out his next words in a deeper, huskier voice. "I saved Sophie's life, the night she was attacked. I couldn't tell you then be-ughhh-because we didn't know who was trying to kill her then. I had to keep Sophie safe. I tried... but in the end she saved me." His voice grows rougher, his body shifting before their eyes. "Please... don't let them punish RJ because of me... it's not his fault... *ugh*..." He clutches his stomach, his fingers cracking and extending into claws. "Sophie's sister... Nikki! She's the one behind all of this. That's who Sophie is after now! Please believe me… I… *grrrr*…" His eyes flash and his clothes become a pile of shredded cloth as his wolf springs free of its two-legged prison, his growl turning into a howl as he succumbs to the wolf inside of him.

Tim and Andy take several steps back, slowly, but unlike Kensington in the van, there was an almost familiar look in Korban's eyes as he gazed to them with a Wolven face. Tim's hand was on his gun, but Korban's wolf- a great grey beast- simply considered them with a knowing look in his eyes, making no threatening move to attack. His ears and head flick in the direction where Sophie had bolted to chase down the escaping SUV. The massive grey wolf turns to look, just in time to hear the squealing shriek of brakes, followed by the tell-tale crunch of twisting metal that made his stomach sink. Korban's wolf becomes a blur as he rushes toward the sound of the crash, leaving them with some answers and even more questions in his wake.

18: NO TURNING BACK

The forced transformation left him more sore than exhilarated, but when it is over instead of falling into darkness he finds himself once again in control of his wolf. It is strange to view the night with his Wolven eyes without the glow of the full moon, even stranger to find himself outside, the soft, damp grass beneath his massive paws in place of solid concrete. He was not in his familiar den of brick and steel, shielded from the world. Instead he was free of any cage that could hold him back. It was frightening and liberating.

He sees his two human friends stepping away from him and back towards the car. He'd lost them when he ran from the hospital to follow Sophie's scent, but somehow they were able to catch up with him. Too late to stop Sophie from getting shot, too late to witness Nikki's cruel revelation or Matt's attempt to shoot him.

The toxin that had triggered his transfiguration without the wild moon's call remained only as several dark drops in the discarded dart near his paws. The same dart he had plunged into himself after yanking it from the ground where it had narrowly missed him, choosing to join Sophie in her fate. He gazes to Tim and Andy, watching as Andy's hand goes to his holstered gun, fingers trembling. He tries to apologize but no sound comes from his elongated muzzle.

For a brief moment time seems to stand still, until the sound of screeching brakes followed by a crash of metal comes from up the road.

There are no words to express his apology or to say anything else to the two human police officers who stood there. Korban lunges into a sprint, his feet kicking the earth beneath him as he races toward the wreck. His nostrils flare as he rushes towards the smell of gasoline, smoke, and blood. When he arrives at the scene of the accident mere seconds later his heart is racing. The SUV is twisted and bent, almost unrecognizable as dark smoke plumes from where the engine had been. There are tracks on the road leading to where the vehicle had collided with the side of an ill-fated train bridge. There is the smell of burning polyester, plastic, and flesh that makes his stomach churn.

He catches the scent of mint, vanilla and wolf and turns, seeing the familiar golden werewolf as she snarls and paces, keeping her distance as flames rise from the wreckage. Sophie bares her teeth as she growls at the wreck and doesn't notice him at first, or is too focused on her prey to be bothered by him. He trots over to her side and she snaps at him, her eyes wild and enraged. In the distance the wail of sirens pierced the air. If they were caught he knew they would never be free again. There were no second chances if you broke the rules, and the thought of being trapped in this form forever was not as frightening to him as being stuck as a Wolven then locked away in quarantine for the rest of his days. He bares his teeth as he growls at Sophie, her ears flattening and hackles raised.

The sirens were growing in numbers and volume, and time was running out. Korban tackles her and the two werewolves roll and snap at one another, moving away from the remains of the SUV. Sophie claws and struggles back, getting in several sharp bites into him as they tussle toward the lake. She draws blood when she sinks her fangs into his leg and he yelps, causing her to draw back quickly, and for a moment she pauses, staring at him as though seeing him for the first time.

The emergency vehicles arrive, brakes screeching and causing both wolves to flatten their ears. In the blue and red lights, Korban watches as Sophie growls and starts towards the response team as they rush to put out the blaze. He steps in front of her with a growl of his own, warning her not to go after them without words. She snaps at him in response but doesn't move toward the people again. Instead she suddenly bolts, running along the lake's edge at lightning speed, moving far away from the crash scene.

Korban tears off after her, following her over the marshy banks of the lake until they reached the paved trails that circled the surrounding park. The ground is hard and rough against his paws and reminds him of home as he rushes towards her scent, wild vanilla and mint and fear intertwined with the heavenly musk of her wolf. Her fear is so thick he can taste it and he surges forward as he follows her path.

The solid, black asphalt beneath his paws gives way to more worn stones, some rough on his feet. Still he follows her, ignoring the sharp pokes and catches a glimpse of her golden fur as she streaked around the curve of the trail. She leads him across a thankfully dark and quiet stretch of road, where she suddenly stills to a stop and sniffs the air. He is almost caught up to her when he hears it – a young man's voice, tight and high with fear, "N-nice doggy…"

Sophie's ears remain flat and her lip curls as a low growl emerges. Her heart is still pounding, her hackles raised at this new threat. Before she can pounce, Korban catches up with a panting snort, returning her attention on her pursuer and causing her to yelp in surprise before bolting again. He finds himself running alongside her, until she snaps at him and he slows to the point of flanking her. They move away from the road and through a patch of houses and small buildings, over and past railroad tracks. In the distance there are lights, rumbling tracks and a whistle that is a mere echo of the sound from before, yet it urges both of them forward, further away from civilization.

Sophie trots over the last set of tracks, dodging a stopped set of train cars and heading up between a cluster of trees. He continues to move alongside her, keeping with her pace even as his tongue began to loll out of the side of his mouth. As they moved deeper and deeper into the woods her fear began to fade and in its place something else takes hold of both of them. Freedom.

All the pain and fear faded away as they put the roads and buildings behind them and slipped deeper into the wild. No longer did the rough pavement scrape his paws, the damp dirt and grass soothing their aching feet. Running became less of a necessity and more of an exhilaration. They flowed like water through the thickening trees and brush, breezing past creeks and streams, sloshing over a shallow river and pausing to lap up the cool water together. She keeps her gaze on him when they pause and studies him warily for a long moment. The last of her fear subsides and in that moment he watches her eyes bleed from red to amber again.

She approaches him then, warily at first, but then her ears lift along with her tail. He remains still as she comes near and sniffs at his collar. His heart races and he feels her moist breath tickle the skin under his fur. She bows her head down and licks at his healing leg bite in apology and he snorts and buries his nose into her furry neck in turn with a forgiving huff.

A soft gust of wind ruffles their fur and carries the scents of the forest- fragrant pine, wet grass and animal musk. Strange and new smells, so very different from the ones that were associated with home. Still, these new fragrances were invigorating and felt right. Together they run into the night, deeper into the forest, putting miles between them and civilization. Far, far away from the dangers of the human world, where the monsters hid in plain sight.

As the sun rose and the night bled away into day they remained on four legs. It seemed without the full moon to lull the beast back into its cage they were stuck as wolves, but there were far worse things. Especially now, Korban thinks to himself as he and Sophie run free, out into the wild forest where no human had roamed for years. His heart soars. They were together, and for now that was more than enough for him. Together they had already proven they were a team- no, not a team.

A pack. Safe even in uncharted territory.

~*~

Hungry for more?

Sophie and Korban's adventure is only beginning!

To be continued in *Captured Moonlight*, book two of the

Tainted Moonlight Series!

COMING SOON

~*~

JOIN THE PACK TODAY

Check out the official website taintedmoonlightbook.com for updates, character biographies, and more bonus content!

~*~

ACKNOWLEDGMENTS

There are so many amazing people to thank who have helped me on my journey, enough to fill a novel of its own, but I'll do my best to name those who guided me on my way. Thank you first and foremost to my parents and stepparents, for being my first fans and always believing in me no matter what my creative pursuit has been. I love you Mom and Dad. Thank you as well to my family and friends for your endless love and support. To all of my teachers and professors, thank you all for giving me the tools, confidence, and inspiration. RJ is my tribute to each and every one of you.

A special nod to those who helped me with my fact checking- to Tyler for helping me find my way around a vehicle and Cassandra for the forensics information that helped bring another level of realism into my fantasy world. To one of my very first readers, Kristin, thank you as well for helping me with the medical facts and information as well- you are going to make one amazing doctor sis.

There are some people who I simply cannot thank enough, including Jim and Connie, who literally kept a roof over my head while I pursued my dreams. Thank you so much for everything you have done for me. To my Angel sisters, Shine sisters, and OWLs, you know who you are, but special thanks to Marie Dees, Elizabeth, Whitney, German, and Jessica for the hours spent at Barney's and the gallons of coffee and tea that fueled this book (as well as many of yours!). I can't forget to thank fellow author Nicholas T. Davis for all of your help as well when it came to publishing this story, thank you and see you at karaoke! Also to Dave, one of my most unexpected and sweetest friends from high school, thank you for your help and praise through the years, and I hope you found my little nod for you in my story. Thanks to your cousin as well for giving me my first critical feedback during the earlier drafts, thanks to her I was able to make this story even better than I had originally imagined it to be.

An honorable mention to my friends who helped support my story through preordering it on Inkshares, though that did not kick off my story I got a snapshot of how many people cared to help bring my story into the light. To Derrick, Nicholas, Uncle Miles, Adriaan, Kari, Fay, Godfrey, Bree, Larry and Candace Disotell, Uncle Gary, Gregory, Michelle, RuthAnn, Nicole, Jackie, Ed, Kathie, Kristen, Eva, Jill and Becca. If I forgot to put your name here and you preordered, I apologize, there were dozens of you and I appreciate all the help you provided me for the first round of this publishing adventure. Thank you all again for your support!

Last but definitely not least, a very special thank you to those who helped me polish off this project. My beloved friends and beta readers, who were the first to read this and gave me feedback- Dawn (who read it first, and read it twice!), Carrie (who gave me wonderful advice on how to make improvements, as well as many wonderful tips on what to watch to be inspired), Adam (for pointing my fine tooth comb in the right direction for the final edit) and last but not least, my best friend for over a quarter century, Tina. LYLAS and thank you for everything you have ever done. Our many adventures (and many more to come!) have inspired me and made me the woman and writer I am today. Thank you for being there through the storms and sunshine.

And thank you, the reader who is finishing this first novel. I hope I have not let you down. I hope that you will continue to enjoy the journey of Korban and Sophie as they grow and develop more in this series. I have so much planned and I look forward to sharing more of their story and world with you!

Until the next book be well and never give up on your dreams. Time and time again, as cliché as it may sound, they will come true. What they don't always say is that it takes hard work and dedication to get there, but when you do- believe me, it is so worth it.

ABOUT THE AUTHOR

Erin Kelly lives in Syracuse, New York with two loving cats, a precocious Siamese, and a wacky Westie named Winchester after one of her favorite television series. When she is not writing about werewolves, she is often drawing, reading, swimming at the gym, or can be found at several local karaoke bars belting out ballads by the Backstreet Boys with her friends.

Made in the USA
Middletown, DE
17 September 2017